Top Ten Uses for an Unworn Prom Dress

Top Ten Uses for an Unworn Prom Dress

a novel by

Tina Ferraro

Delacorte Press

Published by Delacorte Press
an imprint of Random House Children's Books
a division of Random House, Inc.
New York

www.randomhouse.com/teens

Educators and librarians, for a variety of teaching tools, visit us at
www.randomhouse.com/teachers

Library of Congress Cataloging-in-Publication Data
Ferraro, Tina.
Top ten uses for an unworn prom dress / Tina Ferraro.—1st ed.
p. cm.
Summary: Having been stood up for prom the previous year, high school junior
Nicolette works on a top ten list of things to do with her unworn dress while also
trying to help her divorced parents and take care of her relationships
with her best friend and with potential boyfriends.
ISBN 978-0-385-73368-7 (tr pbk)—ISBN 978-0-385-90383-7 (glb)
[1. Interpersonal relations—Fiction.   2. Family problems—Fiction.
3. Proms—Fiction.   4. High schools—Fiction.   5. Schools—Fiction.]
I. Title.
PZ7.F365Top 2007
[Fic]—dc22

2006004991

The text of this book is set in 12-point Apollo MT.
Book design by Angela Carlino

Printed in the United States of America
10 9 8 7 6 5 4 3 2 1

First Edition

With heartfelt thanks to my agent, Nadia Cornier; my editor, Krista Marino; my critique partners, Kelly Parra and Cheryl Mansfield; my plot doctors, Terri, Sandi, Lindsey, and my daughter, Sarah; my sons, Patrick and Nick; and my parents, for starting me on my writing journey.

For Robert,
who helped make all my
dreams come true

Top Ten Uses for an Unworn Prom Dress

Prom Goddess

A heavenly floral scent surrounds me as the zipper of The Dress magically closes against my back. I gaze at myself in the mirror on the door—which isn't usually there, but *whatever*—and lose myself in the vision. I am totally feminine, elegant even, from the heart-shaped bodice to the nipped-in waistline to the bit of crinoline peeking out from under the hem.

Not a volleyball-induced callus, bruise, or scab to be seen. I am Nicolette Antonovich, Prom Goddess.

My mother is suddenly beside me, mouthing words about *him* being on the doorstep.

Him. Rod "Rascal" Pasqual, the big blond football player who asked me to his junior prom. Who needed a date when his longtime girlfriend up and moved out of state. And who is so far out of my league that I suspect some of my bruises are from pinching myself.

Mom and I float through the mirror, down the hall, through the living room, and to the front door. Which seems to be opening with a will of its own.

Rascal's too-handsome face is right in front of me. His lips move, but his words are out of sync, something about me looking fantastic. I want to tell him it's all for him, but my own voice gets drowned out.

By laughter. High-pitched screeches and cackles— like the Wicked Witch of the West has been cloned and is laughing her heart out on my front lawn.

Then there are faces, everywhere. All around Rascal. And laughing. My teammates, my best friend, her evil brother. And inside the circle of Rascal's arms, I see someone. It's his perfect girlfriend, back where she belongs.

And zapping me—and the world's most beautiful prom dress—back into our places, too. Namely, the bedroom. In front of the mirror. Alone.

Just Say Yes

My mouth was gaping when I woke up this morning, but I wasn't laughing. I wasn't screaming. I'm not even sure I was breathing.

That dream—the nightmare—hit *waaay* too close to home. Although in real life, Rascal had given me the courtesy of a before-the-prom, private communication that Kylie had come back to town, the bottom line was still the same. My prom dress and I were left out in the cold and, real or imagined, I was left trying to lose the remnants of laughing faces.

Rascal and his girlfriend. My coach and teammates.

My best friend, Alison, and her seventeen-year-old brother.

Especially her brother. Jared McCreary, who still treated me like I was twelve years old, when he bothered to treat me like anything at all. Yet despite that, I have been continuously forced to humble myself and ask for his help throughout my saga. As I was going to have to do again today—breaking our two-month unacknowledged and mutual silence.

Which was only slightly more appealing than the nightmare I was still slowly shaking off.

And an hour or so later, things were quickly going from bad to worse. Not only did I have to grovel this time, but it looked like I had to do it in front of Jared's buddies. Three idiots so invested in my present humiliation that they probably wouldn't notice if hundred-dollar bills fell from the AC vents.

There I was, standing beside Hillside High School's Senior Bench and staring into the eyes of the one person I swore I'd never ask for anything again.

I steeled my nerves, reminding myself of my desperate crusade: to prevent my mother from potentially losing our house. Our somewhat comfortable way of life. And our frigging minds.

I would suck it up.

Somehow.

I knew the only way I stood a chance with Jared was by playing by his rules. Pretending that the loud, finger-pointing scene on the deck of his parents' Santa Barbara beach house eight weeks ago hadn't happened. After he'd basically pulled me out of the arms of a hunky high school Canadian and then lectured me on safety and judgment.

Like I said—twelve years old.

But for today's purposes, I was determined to give that memory—as well as my dignity—the morning off.

With that in mind, I took a deep breath and forced it out. "I need to hire you." My hands balled at my sides like I meant business, when deep down, all a little voice inside me could say was: *Please. Please. Please.*

It came as no surprise when the guys lounging around him laughed. And a crooked smile tugged at Jared's mouth. Not a particularly wicked smile or even one that lit up his eyes, but his pleasure at my discomfort could not be denied.

"*Hire* me. Who's to say you can *afford* me, Nic?"

His buddies did that nudge-and-smirk thing.

I probably rolled my eyes. I know I did mentally. It was bad enough that the night before I'd had to actually *see* my mom cry instead of just hearing the muffled sobs through the bedroom walls. No self-centered, egomaniacal, year-older brother of my best friend was going to scare me into going through that again. I was determined.

"Oh?" I said, trying to make light of it. "How much you selling yourself for these days?"

A couple of "oooh"s and a "She got you, dude!" sounded from the peanut gallery.

Jared slid off the bench and stood to his full almost

six feet, clearly meaning to intimidate little old me. But considering I was the only volleyball starter under 5'2" in the history of Hillside High School, you'd think he'd know I didn't let size get to me. Or a challenge, for that matter.

Besides, *that* was something I had more experience with than the McCrearys. Jared and his sister, Alison, had a pretty cinchy life. Not that I didn't adore Alison. She had a huge heart and was always there for me. It was her brother who got under my skin.

But it was also her brother, and his vintage '71 Chevy Camaro, that I needed more than I'd ever like to admit.

"Listen," I said, and flicked my head toward the stairwell. "Walk me down to my locker and we'll come up with something that benefits us both."

His buddies (the Three Stooges? Musketeers? Blind Mice?) did these stupid high fives.

"Ben-e-fits," the guy named Kevin or Keith called out. "I don't think she's talking about *money*, Jared!"

Guys could be so charming.

Jared followed me down the stairs and into the first-floor corridor, as I'd suspected he would. In these first six weeks of school, we might have not so much as nodded in each other's direction, but I knew he was a decent guy and would at least hear me out.

"So?" he said, stopping beside me when we got to my locker.

"I need to go see my father," I said, and popped my lock open. Then met his gaze. Yep, there was a frown.

"I thought you hated him."

"Right now my needing him is more important than my hating him."

I couldn't help drawing the parallel between my two current situations with the male sex.

"Where's he living again?"

"Ventura," I answered, which we both knew was an hour's drive north of our Los Angeles community, in the best of traffic.

"We're talking rush hour?"

"Depends when we go. But right after school works for me."

"Okay," he said simply.

"Okay?" I couldn't believe it was so easy.

He nodded.

"Well, good. So how much you charging?"

I studied his face. Dark eyes. Arched brows. And that thick chestnut-brown hair. There had been moments when I'd have given my right arm to trade my blond fluff for his glossy waves. But then, without an arm, I'd probably still struggle in the looks department.

"What'd you pay me last time?"

"Eight an hour," I said. "Plus gas." It wasn't like I could ask Jared to be seen with me in his passenger seat for less than minimum wage, but this was precisely the problem. Money.

He nodded, then glanced away from me. At the far end of the hallway, coming into focus, were Kylie Shoenbacher and her entourage. Or what Alison and I called the Pretty Parade. Four or five of them, gliding in perfect synchronization, led by the roll of Kylie's painted eyes, her slender hips, and the bouncity-bounce of her B cups.

Kylie and I were as different as night and day, she being beautiful, stylish, and popular, me being . . . well . . . can I get back to you on that?

I mean, I wasn't a total loser or anything. Just small, in both height and feminine curves, light on the talent with makeup, and had long ago given up on taming my tight, curly hair. (Suffice to say I worshipped at the altar of barrettes and hair ties.) And even when money *hadn't* been an issue, I had never been interested in manicures or designer sunglasses, so I'd never be Kylie's idea of a quality girl.

But whether we liked it or not, she and I shared a bit of history. June 10 of the last school year. When I was a sophomore and she was a junior. And she went to the prom with my date.

I trained my gaze on Jared, who seemed, at that moment, preferable to Kylie.

"So," I said to him, trying to appear as laid-back as possible. "When can we go?"

A shift in the air told me the Parade had cruised on by. Jared threw a fleeting look at the retreating wall of wiggles, and I turned, too, half expecting to see handfuls of confetti and hard candy falling in their wake.

He glanced back at me. "You're the lady with the bankroll. When do you want to go?"

Now would be good. Just cruise out the side door, jump in his car, and drive away from my problems.

But first things first. I still had fifth and sixth

period. I had to talk Coach Luther into letting me skip a practice (about as easy as escaping a maximum-security prison). I needed to call Dad (always a highlight). And then there was the lie I needed to concoct for Mom so she wouldn't get suspicious, setting her up for the bigger lie I'd tell when I got back.

And all this went under the guise of making things better?

"Tomorrow?" I asked.

"That works."

"I'll have to call you tonight. After I talk to my dad."

"You know the number." He took a couple of steps away, then stopped and turned back toward me. "Oh, and I'll tell Keith and those guys that you're paying me, but no promises that they'll listen."

"Why are you even friends with them?"

"I've known them forever. Besides, it won't hurt your rep much. Extra Small and the Extra-Hot Senior."

I drew a long inhale. "Extra Small" was something he'd lovingly attached to me when he found out I'd been given that size for my eighth-grade promotion picnic T-shirt. Double meanings and put-downs totally intended, of course.

He was halfway to the staircase before I found something sharp to throw.

"You drop this pen?"

The deep, familiar voice caught me off guard. I looked up into Rascal's eyes. Blue and gorgeous.

Talk about extra-hot seniors! With dark blond hair

and high cheekbones, on his worst days he was merely gorgeous. On his best, he could pass for a younger brother of Heath Ledger.

Anytime now I'd be developing that immunity my mother talked about. The one where I'd realize Rascal was a complete jerk and never should have asked me to the prom when he had a girlfriend—whether or not she'd been living out of state.

Yep, any day now . . .

"Or," he continued, "did you actually throw this thing at McCreary?"

"Yeah, I threw it," I said, and managed to finagle the pen back without too much skin-on-skin action. "He deserved it."

"Give me the word, Nicolette," he said, and pounded a fist into his palm. "And I'll take care of him for you."

I scoffed. Even though he had ripped my heart out, I could still totally get my mind around the vision of him with his shirt off, pecs flexed.

"Come on," he urged, as if I'd really agree.

"I don't want you to fight anyone for me." I felt a smile tug at my mouth. "But I still wouldn't have a problem with you paying me back for my prom dress."

Dimples pressed into his cheeks. He and I had been down this road before—on the last day of school last June, and several times lately, since classes had picked up again. "Don't girls re-wear those dresses as brides-maids or something?"

I blew out a breath. "There's no use for an unworn prom dress, Rascal. Although believe me, I'm working on it."

For real.

Mom and I had a list tacked up on the refrigerator: TOP TEN USES FOR AN UNWORN PROM DRESS. Her idea of using humor as medicine. A heck of a lot better than my way of coping, by leaving that dress on the back of my door so I'd have to look at it every morning and every night, a thorny reminder of what Rascal really was.

So far, the refrigerator list was pretty much blank. It had numbers, starting with ten and counting backward. Apparently David Letterman always saves the best for last.

Sort of like how Rascal was saving me? For when things finally fizzled out with Kylie?

Ha, ha. Dream on, Nic. . . .

"Well, you change your mind about McCreary?" Rascal said, leaning in close, his breath playing hot against my cheek. "You know where to find me."

I choked out a laugh, which was kind of hard with my voice catching in my throat. I wanted to say the same: *You change your mind about Kylie, and you know where to find me.*

But that *so* wasn't coming out. So I stepped back, away from the aura of Rascal's warmth—and into a hard, well-muscled wall.

Ack.

Even though Jared had walked off minutes ago, had

not entered my field of vision, and had absolutely *zero* reason to be anywhere near my body space, I nevertheless knew *he* was the wall.

"McCreary," Rascal said, staring over my head and confirming my suspicions.

"Rascal," Jared answered—but instead of looking at Rascal, he was turned to me. "I forgot," Jared mumbled, thrusting a slip of ripped loose-leaf my way. "Here's my cell phone number. In case I'm out tonight."

I slipped the number into the back pocket of my shorts, then looked up to see the guys' gazes drilling into each other. I half expected them to start circling and sniffing like dogs.

"You're calling *him* tonight?" Rascal asked me, although you'd hardly know it from the way his gaze seared into Jared's.

I nodded, though no one was looking at me. "I—" Then I realized what I had started to do . . . to explain myself to Rascal. The guy who'd left me and my dress without a date for the prom.

I don't think so.

I chewed on the inside of my cheek to stop myself.

Not that Rascal even noticed my nonresponse. He was too busy making this back-of-his-throat noise. For an insane moment, I thought he might throw a punch after all. (And I mean insane because any acts of aggression on our zero-tolerance campus meant automatic suspension, sometimes expulsion.)

Jared shuffled in closer to Rascal, as if accepting an unspoken challenge.

A flutter exploded in my gut. "Okay, you guys," I said, and forced out a laugh. "Whatever's happening here, deal with it after school."

Neither moved. Not a twitch.

So I did. I grabbed my books, slammed my locker, and walked off. I had an agenda. A class about to start. A mother to protect. A father to confront. And a life to fix (or totally ruin, depending on how you wanted to look at it).

Mirror, Mirror

In my weakest moments, when I was about to admit that my mother was right about Rascal and that I was throwing away moments of "the best years of my life" mourning over a buttwipe (my word, not hers), I fell back on his half-baked apology for breaking our date, to keep hope alive that someday, somehow we'd get together.

It had come almost two weeks after the prom, on the last day of my sophomore year. . . .

I'd stayed to talk with Coach Luther about the starter setter position. I'd let her know I was ready to give my all to volleyball (since my love life was a total goose egg—although I didn't tell her *that*). She'd responded that my "all" wasn't good enough, that she'd expect 110 percent. In which case, the position was mine for the taking.

I'd practically danced down the empty hallway. I'd slid my locker combos into place, opened the door, and frozen. Somehow I'd managed to amass a solid block of *stuff* in nine months' time.

Twenty minutes and a trash can later, I'd slung my backpack on. It was crammed with sweatshirts, Tupperware containers, spiral notebooks, romance novels, and four or five umbrellas—I had all I could do to keep myself upright.

As I'd stepped out the side door, early summer rain had pattered down on me. While I was trying to extract an umbrella from my backpack, a forest green minivan had pulled up beside me.

"Get in."

Rascal's voice had set off bells and whistles in my head. Nerve endings I didn't even know I had sprang to life. But oddly, so did some latent brain cells.

Get in. *Get in?* As if he'd said "Jump" and I'd asked "How high?"

"I don't think so," I said, springing one of the umbrellas to life over my head.

"Get in," he said again. Softer this time, idling the van beside me. "You've got all that stuff. I'll take you home."

I'd kept my chin elevated and my pace steady.

"Nicolette. Look . . ." He'd rolled along slowly beside me. "Everything that happened with the prom . . . We never really got to talk."

That was what had stopped my clock. Was an apology possibly in the air? Had he and Kylie split up? Did he want ME to be the bikini-clad girl on his arm that summer?

"Come on," he'd said, and flashed those dimples.

I'd closed the umbrella, heaved the backpack into the rear compartment, and slipped into the bucket seat beside him. "Okay," I said. "Talk."

He'd raced out into traffic, telling me about a summer job he had lined up, and a trip up the coast. Then he'd made what felt like an impulsive turn into one of those drive-thru coffee places and ordered two café mochas. After paying, he'd driven to a parking lot for a nearby home-improvement store. Parked. Motioned for me to take a cup. And then looked everywhere but at me.

"Okay, listen," he began. "About the prom. I admit when I asked you, we barely knew each other. And if Kylie hadn't come back . . ." He threw a look at me, which I caught, then let go. "But she did come back. You know?"

I knew. Oh, did I know.

I'd been the proud owner of The Dress for about forty-eight hours when Alison arrived on my doorstep— gasping for air—to say she'd just seen Kylie with Rascal at a red light. At school the next morning, he'd pulled me aside to say Kylie was back to finish her junior year, which of course put him in a tight spot as far as the prom went.

Three more days passed (long, hopeful days) before he gave me the final word. He was taking Kylie. He had to. She *was* his girlfriend, after all.

"If I'd known she was coming back," he'd said in the van that day, "I never would have asked you."

I'd studied his face, willing him to the next level. To a sentence that included the word "sorry." When that didn't happen, I decided to force his hand. "So you're saying you're sorry?"

He'd shrugged a shoulder.

"So sorry you're going to pay me back for the dress I never got to wear?"

"Hey, I bought you a mocha," he answered, and flashed the smile. "Besides, I half expected to see you at the prom with some other guy."

"I'm still a sophomore," I said. "At least, I was until about an hour ago."

"McCreary's in my year. He could have taken you."

Jared? That was sure out of left field.

Anyway, as an athlete, I knew when to play offense and when to retreat. This had been one of those back-off moments. I'd gotten about as much out of Rascal as he was capable of giving. I had to quit while I was ahead. (Or at least more ahead than behind.)

He'd dropped me off at home, and the entire summer had slipped away before our paths crossed again.

Leaving me ample opportunity to rewrite our past and fantasize a future—in and around occasional bursts of glad-to-be-rid-of-him clarity.

It was safe to say that when it came to Rascal and getting on with my life, I was still a work in progress. . . .

Which sort of explained why I was standing in my bedroom now, transforming myself from a starting setter to a behind-closed-doors prom queen. The conversation with Rascal (and maybe vestiges of last night's dream) had fogged over my brain. And there was only one remedy.

The Dress was pink organza, called "cotton candy" by the owner of the vintage clothing store where I found it. Strapless, the top almost looked heart-shaped from the way it was tapered in at the waist, and the fabric was embroidered with tiny roses that covered miles and miles of crinoline.

Thoughts of Audrey Hepburn in *Roman Holiday* had floated through my mind while the shop owner had mumbled that she didn't remember seeing the dress on the rack before.

Now, think what you will, but the word "magic" *did* come to mind. What it did for my curveless, shapeless figure was otherworldly.

Or at least it had seemed to me that day last June, with Alison beaming at me in the dressing room mirror, and Jared out in his white Camaro, probably dozing because that had been, like, the tenth shop I'd paid him to drive me to.

Without hesitation, I'd forked over every last cent of the money my grandmother had left me.

And for what?

So The Dress would hang behind my door like last year's backpack? So I could wear it to my junior prom this upcoming June, with some friend of a friend or lab partner as my date? Or as part of a group who went dateless for a Girls' Night Out?

Or for moments like this, when I zipped myself inside the pink perfection and gazed into the mirror in secret admiration. I was beginning to feel like Snow White's stepmom—developing a close relationship with the mirror and all.

Slow-dancing to pity party songs in my head, I imagined my hands locking around Rascal's waist. Then traveling up around his neck.

I sang to myself, trying to do my best Paul McCartney.

My dream hands broke from their locked position around his make-believe neck, roamed forward. To his throat. Where they started to squeeze his jugular—

See why my mom wanted me to start up that list? I seriously needed to try to make light of things.

I dropped my hands, real and imaginary, and plopped down on my polka-dot bedspread, the beautiful skirt of my dress making a whooshing sound beneath me.

Why was I torturing myself this way? That prom was ancient history.

What I really needed to do was take the stupid

thing off and donate it to Goodwill. Maybe somebody out there could actually get to wear it outside her bedroom.

But I was stalling. As soon as I defrocked, I'd have to call my dad and try to break the ice. Ask him how he'd been these past couple of months, since neither of us had bothered to pick up the phone.

Maybe I'd sit just a little bit longer.

Top Ten Uses for an Unworn Prom Dress

#10

Create a human-sized nest in which to hide from the world—primarily people you'd rather not be related to.

"Nicolette!" Mom called down the hall. "Dinner!"

A crazy surge of embarrassment shot through me, though it was impossible to tell whether it was from getting caught in The Dress—or the singing and dancing.

I poked my head out of the door and called that I'd be there in a minute . . . once I'd replaced the silky garment in its plastic bag and neatly covered the tracks of my madness. But I didn't say that second part out loud.

•

In the old days—when my dad was still with us—Mom had been a Martha Stewart wannabe. A woman who decorated for every holiday that Hallmark made a card for, cooked meals from scratch, didn't believe in giving store-bought gifts.

On top of that, she truly enjoyed having my friends over, stirring up pitchers of lemonade, playing endless board games. One time she told me she would have loved to have had more kids, and then her voice had drifted. . . .

I had thought for the longest time that she meant it simply hadn't happened. Until I was old enough to realize the real problem: Dad.

Bruce Antonovich. The computer whiz who'd spent the first part of my life either "at the office" or in front of a screen. Who'd encouraged Mom to quit her job as a receptionist when I was born, to stay home with me full-time. And, as she and I independently discovered as the years went by, so she'd be there all the time that he was not.

Dad. Yeah, what a guy.

But oh, it gets better. Much better.

So when I was, like, twelve, there was this new woman at Dad's work. Cathleen Monterey, with slick dark hair and, as it turns out, the slick trick of getting what she wanted. In this case, it was Dad. (God knows why—he was, like, forty, graying, and lived in his own universe half the time. But there's no accounting for taste.) A few weeks before my thirteenth birthday, he packed up his laptops, grabbed a handful of his mini–Almond Joys, and left.

The next thing we know, Cathleen, aka "Caffeine," so called because of her raging intensity and bitter aftertaste, suddenly goes all fat.

And then—what do you know?—I've got a half sister.

So, that's bad enough, right? No . . . no . . . Dad goes and pulls the ultimate whammy. He "puts his career on hold" to stay home with the brat. I believe it's called paternity leave or something. He starts doting over little Autumn (who is fittingly named after the season in which her mother is known to fly around on her broomstick) and pretty much becomes absolutely everything to her that he's never been to me.

Bitter much? Me?

And probably worst of all is the effect it has had on Mom. She always puts on these cheery smiles and tries to tell me that she'll eventually come to terms with it all. But as I believe I mentioned earlier, there's been a lot of crying going on behind closed doors.

After getting her realtor's license, Mom proudly stopped taking alimony from Dad. She decided she would only take child support, so for the past two years she's clomped out of the house every weekday morning in business suits and no-nonsense pumps. But in addition to appearing professional, she looks ten years older now, with extra weight, and these worry lines around her eyes and across her forehead.

But every time things start to get a little gloomy, she becomes this kind of rah-rah cheerleader. Which was what I'd expected last night, when she'd been flipping through the mail during dinner and opened the envelope marked SECOND NOTICE. But instead of a forced hundred-watt beam and some random suggestion like we have mint chip ice cream for dessert, she had burst into tears.

She actually admitted she'd gotten behind on the mortgage. That she hadn't closed so much as a rental lease in at least three months, and there wasn't much in the works. She didn't know how she'd manage to catch up anytime soon.

I didn't have to be a straight-A student to understand we could lose the house. That we'd have to move to an apartment somewhere. And that there simply *were* no apartment buildings in our school district.

Which meant me getting kicked out of overcrowded Hillside High School. Off the volleyball team. Losing Alison. Losing contact with kids I'd gone to school with my whole life. And okay . . . abandoning any teeny, tiny hope of wearing The Dress to Rascal's senior prom instead of his junior.

The whole thing made my head swim. . . .

The whole thing made me *furious* at my father.

And that is why my plan had been hatched and why I was now standing in the kitchen holding the phone to my ear.

My heart did this bing-bang thing when his deep voice answered. No matter how extreme my hatred for him, part of me wanted him to sound totally overjoyed at the sound of my voice, and say something like "I was just telling Cathleen how much smarter and cuter you were at Autumn's age."

Hey, a girl could dream.

Instead, he paused, and I wondered for a devastated moment if he was trying to place my name and voice.

But it was raw concern that whipped back at me. "Is everything all right?"

Oh, God, if only I could answer that honestly!

"Yeah," I said instead, realizing it had been such a long time since I'd called that he probably had a right to wonder. "I just wanted to know if you're going to be home after school tomorrow." And then I all but kicked myself. Would Dad even know what hour constituted after school? "Like four, four-thirty? I was wondering . . . if I could come by?"

Another silence followed, one that shimmered across the telephone line between us. I imagined Dad calculating Autumn's nap schedule, or perhaps trying to reschedule a vital playdate with another two-year-old. I mean, we're talking earth-shattering stuff here.

"Sure," he finally said. "That works. How are you getting here?"

"Alison's brother, Jared."

That didn't seem to faze him, although I wondered if he even remembered My-Best-Friend-Since-I-Was-Twelve or knew she *had* a brother.

"Okay. Anything I should know ahead of time?"

Yeah, I take cash or checks.

"Like," he went on, filling the empty air, "will you and your friend be staying for dinner?"

"No, we'll need to get back."

"Okay. Well, I look forward to seeing you tomorrow, Nicki."

Irritation rose up inside me. But I mumbled something similar, then hung up. I took a few steps into the living room and fell into Mom's blue and white plaid rocker-recliner.

Nicki.

God, that name clawed at me. My little-kid name. From, like, elementary school. No one called me that anymore. No one who was *in* my life, at least.

And he was "looking forward to seeing" me? Say what? If I hadn't called tonight, he probably would have gone days without even thinking about me.

"Nicolette? Honey?"

My mom interrupted my thoughts, calling out from the back of the house.

I worked to find my voice, my composure. "Yeah?"

"Can you bring me a bath towel?"

I swallowed hard. "Sure."

I took a big breath and made my way to the hallway linen closet. Passing over the towels that had been around so long that Dad might have actually used them, I settled for a firm beach towel Alison had brought me from Hawaii. Not exactly what Mom wanted, but all I could bring myself to touch.

"Here, Mom," I said as I slid it through the opening.

She called out her thanks and closed the door.

I had just enough time to make my other phone call. To the other guy I really didn't feel like talking to, or spending time with.

I punched in the McCreary house line first—whether it was out of laziness or habit, I didn't know. When Alison answered, I filled her in, but when she asked how it had felt to speak with my dad . . . I clammed up. Which was weird. I didn't do that with her. She didn't do that with me. We were all about honesty and "being there" for each other's feelings.

But in the back of my mind, I think I knew that repeating Dad's parting line would make it more . . . real. So I just laughed and told her it was about as much fun as a math test.

We made plans to meet up during morning break; then she told me to try Jared's cell phone because he'd gone to the print shop.

(The print shop?)

I took the number from her, figuring it was easier than reaching for my jeans in my gym bag. And faster. I'd get my dirty work done as quickly as possible.

He answered on the first ring, his voice loud against a drone of background noise.

"It's Nicolette," I announced, holding the phone away from my ear.

"Yeah," he yelled. "Are we still on for tomorrow?"

"If it works for you." Wherever he was, the noise was deafening.

"Meet me at my car after sixth period. I park on that side street off the north gate."

Meet him off campus? Of course. God knows he couldn't be seen at my locker or walking the halls with me two days in a row, or rumors might start up that we were actually friends. Imagine what *that* would do for his rep.

"Yeah, okay."

"What?"

"Oh-kay!"

"I'll need gas."

"We'll have time."

"I meant," he yelled, "make sure you bring money."

For lack of a better response, I laughed, though I doubted he heard it over the grinding machinery. Then I called out a loud "See ya later" and disconnected.

Before I ended up with a headache as big as the dread I had about tomorrow.

Checking Out
the Sights

There's one thing I want to make clear: I *did* have a boyfriend once. A real one. Who called me and kissed me and even took me on dates. We were together the last five weeks of my freshman year, until he went off to be a camp counselor, and to this day, when we pass in the caf or hall or something, we still say hello.

So it wasn't like I was a total freakazoid when it came to guys. (No matter how it looks.)

Alison's dated, too. At one point we'd done this pinkie-swear thing that our friendship would always come first, but I think we both knew it was a form of wishful thinking—the hope that guys could fall for us so hard that we'd actually have to be concerned about something like that.

●

During morning break that next day, we sat on the bleachers and drooled over some particularly hot hotties. Alison was tying her orange-red hair into a ponytail while I made a so-fast-you-barely-heard-it mention of my plans with Jared.

I didn't want to give her any ideas about her brother and me hanging out. In the past, she'd been a buffer when I needed a ride, and I didn't want her imagination to get going and cause a crack in her reality: the collision of two completely separate areas of her life that had no right coming together without her direct involvement.

I know it cracked *my* version of reality. I had no desire to spend any more time with Jared McCreary than I absolutely had to.

I popped open a snack-size bag of Fritos and tilted it toward her. She declined with a shake of her hand, her gaze pinned on the field where a runner was slowing down and stripping off his shirt.

"Too bad camera phones are banned at school," she said wistfully.

I knew I was supposed to laugh, but instead I grunted. I'd been the brunt of that camera phone and wasn't about to let her forget it. "Too bad they aren't banned on the beach, too."

Alison turned, mischief sparkling in her eyes. "You aren't still mad?"

"Mad's not the right word," I said, remembering how she'd told Canadian Guy I'd hold his beer while he futzed with sunblock—even though I totally didn't drink—and then took a quick, incriminating photo of me with the can. She'd laughed, held the phone *waaay* above her head, and said either I became her slave, or she'd e-mail it to Coach Luther.

I'd tried to smile, but the threat had all-too-real implications. Any Hillside athlete who got caught drinking had his or her stupid butt thrown out of sports.

"Anyway, Nic, you know I deleted it."

"Uh-huh."

"I *did*." A smile curled her mouth. "But maybe you want to buy me some cookies at lunch today, just to make sure?"

I swatted her arm and, wanting a radical change of subject, launched into the big BS story I'd told Mom last night. "I waited until she'd turned out her light. Then I called out from my room, like I'd just remembered, 'Oh, Mom, I have to stay late after practice tomorrow. I told Coach Luther I'd help her take down the nets and stuff for the basketball game.' "

Alison's face pinkened as she swallowed a sip of Diet Pepsi, and then she laughed so hard I thought soda might come out her nose. "You know basketball season hasn't started yet, right?"

With anyone but Alison, I might have tried to cover my stupidity. "It hasn't?"

"Seriously!" She laughed and tucked some loose hair behind her ear. "Okay, okay, here's what you do. If you get caught, you claim you said, um, something like badminton. Yeah, that would be good."

"Does our school even have a badminton team?"

"I don't think so. But we've played it in PE. Seriously, you'll never get to that. Because you'll be too busy going off on how she wasn't listening to you. How nobody *ever* listens to you."

"Nobody? That works?"

"Sure does at my house."

"Yeah, well, yours is a lot more crowded." A way bigger place, but her two parents were actually around. "I'll keep that tactic in mind."

"So what big fat lie did you tell the coach?"

Guilt made a sudden appearance in my gut. "Nothing—yet. I'm planning to go to her office instead of the locker room later. I'm going to be 'sick.' " I did little quote marks with my fingers. "Zoe did that once, and Luther let her go home."

"Was she faking it?"

I shrugged. Zoe Zane and I were "team friends." We hung together at practices and on game buses but respected the general rules of casual friendship in that we didn't call just to chat or try to pry info out of each other. "I didn't ask," I said. "All I know is, it worked."

"Then go with it."

I nodded and dumped the last of the Fritos dust and crumbs into my hand, and licked them up.

"I just hope it all goes all right, Nic, that you get the money and everything."

"Yeah. Thanks." I considered asking her to join Jared and me, but then thought better of it. Why would she *want* to go? And why put her in the situation where she had to turn me down?

Alison glanced at her watch, then flicked her head toward the building. "Walk me to my locker? I've got my Spanish presentation, and I don't want to be late."

I rose and slung my backpack over one shoulder. "Come on, doesn't your book tell you how to say 'punctually challenged' *en español*?"

She nudged me in the ribs.

Which is why I was smiling when I looked up. And directly into Rascal's eyes.

His mouth curved and something sparked in his eye, setting off fireworks inside me.

"Hi," I said automatically. And his lovely girlfriend, a few steps behind, looked dead into my eyes. Zapping me with implied threats of bodily harm. One hundred percent *Back off, he's mine* hatred. A world away from her usual bimbacious looks.

Kylie probably didn't remember—or care—but I *had* felt the poison-tipped arrow of her wrath before. Back in middle school, the semester when we'd both worked as servers in the caf. We'd shared a few civil conversations, even a smile or two—until the day she'd shown up, clutching her stomach, claiming to be nauseous.

I'd figured she was faking to spend more time with the then-new hot guy, Rascal, something I totally understood and even sort of applauded. But the caf lady believed Kylie was sick and told me to ladle her a bowl of soup.

I did as instructed, giving Kylie a bit of a wink as I handed it over.

According to school legend, during her next class, Kylie bolted from her seat and made a mad dash for the door. But didn't make it. Soon yellow broth and chunks of pasta and colorful veggies were streaming across the hardwood floor. The whole class thought it was the best thing they'd ever seen. They were hysterical, and apparently it was Rascal's laughter that could be heard all the way down the stairwell.

When Kylie recovered from what turned out to be the stomach flu, she returned with her head held high—and dim-witted allegations against *me*, that I'd poisoned her soup in an attempt to humiliate her. Luckily no one took her seriously, and that was the end of it.

We'd never spoken again, though. I mean, what was there to say?

Rascal was still grinning when he turned back to Kylie now. "Pick up the pace, Chunky."

Chunky. Chunky?

In no world could that girl be considered fat, so it could only mean one thing—a love name. How nice.

•

After school, I headed toward the gym. In an attempt to calm my nerves, I concentrated on volleyball and how much I loved the sport. The pregame excite-

34

ment, the adrenaline rush, the roar of the crowd when our team scored. All really good stuff, which pretty much made up for the grueling workouts and the fact that Luther was such a tyrant that I had to lie to get out of one stupid practice.

My nerves weren't only about my fear of Coach Luther's acid tongue, though. Somewhere between finding out how much college really costs and how little income my parents really had, volleyball had taken on new meaning for me: earning a potential scholarship. Which could put me through college. So I had to be supercareful not to jeopardize my good standing with Luther or my starting center position.

Unfortunately, moments later, I discovered that facing down Coach Luther was harder than I'd expected. *Waaay* harder. I'm an okay liar—I mean, every kid with a parent has experience with truth-twisting, right?—but I think I'd forgotten how steely her gaze could be when she sensed a player *daring* to step out of the Volleyball Box.

A glance at the wall clock told me it was 2:50. I was five minutes late already, so I'd crossed the point of no return. I had better lie and lie *good*.

"Antonovich?" she said, a brow firmly arched. "You are in my doorway instead of the gym . . . *why?*"

"I—I don't feel well," I said, and slumped into the plastic chair beside her desk. I pressed my arm tight against my stomach, and focused my eyes on the speckled tiles beneath my feet. "Cramps."

She was silent for so long I was forced to look up.

"Cramps," she repeated.

After a series of whomp-whomp-whomp heartbeats inside my chest, her voice went all coachlike and severe. "All right. But only this once. I'm not in the habit of babying my players. Next time, take a painkiller and show up ready to work."

"Okay," I managed, and slowly stood up. "Thank you."

"Sometimes players like to pull things over on their coaches, Antonovich," she said, her voice in a more normal register. "But I know you'd never try anything like that. You respect me too much. You respect the game too much."

I nodded. A lot. Then I moved toward the door, remembering to grab my gut. This time I had no problem faking pain. I felt like I'd been sucker punched.

By guilt.

Who's Your Daddy?

Minutes later, I was slipping into Jared's car. "Drive," I said.

"Yes, ma'am!"

He had on a gray T-shirt with some sort of jumbled logo on the front, a loose pair of board shorts, and high-tops. But it wasn't until he climbed out of his car at the gas station that I discovered he was wearing navy blue boxers as well. With little diamonds on them.

More than I wanted to know. Way more.

So why, when he slid back into the car, did I meet his eye and ask about the print shop? Almost like I cared about his personal life?

He gave me one of his usual bored scowls and merged into traffic. "My uncle owns the place. I help out every now and then." I must have looked as surprised as I felt, because he shrugged a shoulder and continued, "Senior year's not that hard. I've done my SATs, and most of the honors courses are behind me. Thought I'd make some pocket money for college."

My thoughts must have still been all over my face, because while pulling onto the freeway ramp, he answered the question that I was fighting not to say out loud. "It'll be nice not to have to hit my dad up for *everything.*"

Okay. So it made sense—slightly.

As we continued north, my stomach began to resemble the hard, sickening ball that I used to feel on Halloween after a long day of eating candy. Which was totally ironic, because I hadn't eaten a chocolate bar since Dad and his mini–Almond Joys had vacated our house.

I did, however, accept a stick of Juicy Fruit when Jared pulled a pack from his glove compartment. My steely mouth needed moistening—and something to do. Funny, though . . . I couldn't remember ever seeing Jared chew gum before.

"What's with the gum?" I had to ask.

"Somebody left it in my car after we left the day-care center job last weekend."

"Out in Sepulveda?" I asked. People from wood shop and several other clubs had donated supplies and energy to help rebuild play equipment lost in a fire.

He nodded. "A bunch of people rode with me."

I imagined that with this Camaro, he'd had to turn riders away. And from Alison's stories about her rule-following brother, he had stayed to the legal limit of one person per seat belt. He wasn't the type to take unnecessary risks, or put himself in the spotlight in any way, for that matter. Like last year, following the spring show, he had gotten a standing ovation. But not for onstage action—for the scenery he'd sawed and painted for the production. Alison told me later that he'd played it down, but their parents had been thrilled.

Parents were like that. At least, the ones who remembered you were alive were.

Which reminded me, I had one more teeny, tiny favor to ask from Jared. "It would be nice," I said, and tried not to wince, "if you came inside my dad's house with me. He'll sort of expect that, since you drove me all the way there."

He paused for a long moment. "What, he doesn't realize you're trading your favors for this ride?"

A smile gleamed in his eye but didn't keep me from giving his upper arm a punch. Which was harder than I'd expected. His muscle, that is. Maybe those saws and hammers were heavier than they looked.

"Ow," he said, tightening his hold on the steering wheel. "Remind me not to spread down-and-dirty rumors about you."

I knew he was joking, but he was less irritating

than when he treated me like a kid—so you take what you can get, right?

And I *had* paid him. Thirty bucks more than covered things.

"So," Jared said. "After the hello? I, what, disappear? I mean, you need time alone to talk about . . . whatever it is you need to talk about, right?"

I nodded. And looked out the window at the ivy-covered freeway walls, the rolling brown hills in the distance. I knew I needed to fess up—I'd probably need him to take me to the bank afterward. It would be so much easier to just get it all done at once.

But Jared was a rich kid. And not a heart-on-his-sleeve rich kid like his sister, who helped organize the school's Thanksgiving food drive, and who one time gave a homeless woman a twenty-dollar bill out of her allowance.

He'd judge me. He'd judge Mom.

I blew out a sigh.

"Yeah," I answered. "If you could hang around for a few minutes, then take off to go get a Coke or something, and wait for me out front. That would be great."

I slumped down in my seat.

●

My dad's house was on a semicircular street of newish two-story houses that all looked the same. Every house had a name written on the mailbox. I half expected the box outside Dad's place to say MIDLIFE CRISIS.

As I moved up his walk, my hands felt fresh-from-the-freezer cold.

Jared's voice cut through my wall of anxiety. "Am I supposed to be, you know, anything more than your driver? Your boyfriend or something?"

It occurred to me to laugh. But my humor had frozen along with my nerves. "Just be you."

I pressed the buzzer and the door opened. Immediately. And there was Dad, like he'd been waiting for me.

My gaze locked with his—squinty blue eyes behind wire-framed glasses—and for a strange moment I went through a quick thaw. He was my dad, after all, the guy who'd let me sit on his lap at dinner, eat the food off his plate. Who'd assured me that thunder wasn't clouds bumping together. Who'd taught me how to float in the pool . . .

Then a noise erupted just below his chin, and my gaze followed.

And there she was. My replacement.

"Nicolette," Dad said, so warmly I was sure that he'd been practicing. Then he actually placed the kid down by his feet and gave me the hug I'd been dreading.

"Hey, Dad," I managed, playing the game, and gave him a squeeze.

He felt warm and strong, and still smelled like a piney aftershave. A good smell. Part of my brain told me I should hate him even more for being so *alive*, rather than a person who'd ceased to exist in my life. But soon enough, the monster made a whining noise, we dropped our arms, and guess who was the center of attention again.

"Hasn't she gotten big?" Dad said, his smile widening. "Two years old last month."

•

The living room was stark beige, and the ceiling went on forever. My mother would have cozied the place up with pillows and dried floral arrangements or something, but obviously Dad was no longer into warm and fuzzy.

We made small talk about the drive and school. So far it was as pleasant as an inner-ear infection. Then Jared excused himself to "go fill up the tank." I wanted to slip out behind him, but he quickly disappeared, and then it was just Dad, the parasite, and me. One big happy family.

Dad zapped on the TV and Autumn slid off his lap and waddled toward the tube, saying something about a character named Dora.

In the perfect version of my life, this would be when my dad and I would have an incredible conversation ending with him begging my forgiveness and handing me a check for, say, the entire balance my mom owed to the bank. Then he'd say that he was leaving Caffeine and their rug rat and coming back to Mom and me.

Because wasn't Dad the one who'd taught me if you were going to dream, to dream big?

His lips pressed together. "So what's up?"

I just went for it. "I need money. Mom's gotten behind on the mortgage and I think the bank's going to take the house."

"What does your mother think?"

The words came out of me in a hollow whisper, the voice of a stranger: "She's scared."

He glanced down.

Then I told him exactly how much I wanted . . . a sum I'd calculated quite fairly, I thought, figuring on this month's payment and last, in the hopes that the clean slate would give Mom the confidence to close a property before the bill came next month.

"Would if I could, kiddo. But I don't have it."

From my Intro to Business class, I recalled lessons on transferring funds, cashing in stocks. Those things took time. "Okay. Well, when *can* you get it to me?"

He leaned forward, his elbows resting on his knees. "I don't think you understand. I don't have the money." Little lines splintered out from his eyes, accentuating his frown, making me think he was telling the truth.

Which was crazy. He'd been a successful computer programmer for more years than I'd been alive. Could he have possibly sunk every penny into this beige castle?

Or was it a lie?

I probably should have just shrugged and walked out. Or played my ace: threaten to move in with them if Mom lost the house.

Instead, with anxiety churning in me so fiercely I could hardly see, I leaned *my* elbows on my knees, and looked him dead in the eye. "If Autumn needed the money, you'd find it for her."

My words hanging in the air, I waited for him to re-act, apologize, make a denial. Something that would give me leverage.

Instead, he knocked the breath right out of me.

"You know," he said, "you're right."

Top Ten Uses for an Unworn Prom Dress

#9

Wad up a fistful of the pristine crinoline and shove it down your father's throat until he gags, chokes, and becomes as stuffed as a Thanksgiving turkey.

I balled my fists at my sides, praying for inner strength. I'd known, deep down, he loved her more, but to hear him admit it, so easily, without shame . . . wow. It hurt a thousand times worse than any spike drill or lap run Coach Luther had ever put me through.

"Autumn is a toddler," my dad went on, all steely-toned and paternal. "The only reason she'd need money would be life and death. Copayment on surgery or something."

I leapt to my feet, tottering a little in my heeled sandals. "This is life and death, too, Dad. Don't you see?

It'll be the end of Mom's sanity and the end of my life as I know it!"

After a long inhale, Dad rose and stared down into my eyes. "And your mother is okay with taking money from me?"

"She has no idea I'm here. I was . . . ," I said, then reminded myself to think positive, "I *am* going to take the money to the bank myself. Then afterward, tell her I deposited what I had left over from the money Grandma left me."

Okay—truth? Grandma's money was long gone, taken out of the ATM in twenty-dollar bills all last year, before I'd blown the rest on The Dress. But I'd known better than to admit all that to Mom, so it was reasonable for her to believe I still had some.

"Look," I said, speaking over the thundering of my heart, trying to sound adult and levelheaded. "You pay Mom the bare minimum of child support. No alimony. You *owe* us this." My voice caught. "You owe me this."

After a moment, he nodded. "You're probably right."

I was?

Well, of course I was!

He disappeared, then returned with a slender check-book and pen. "How about I make it out to the bank?"

I tried to feel joy or triumph, but it was impossible to isolate any one feeling. "Yes, the name—"

"I know. I'm the one who secured the mortgage."

He tore the check out and handed it to me. "Wait until Friday to deposit this. I'll have it covered by then."

I didn't know from where, or how. I didn't really care.

"Take it into the bank yourself. Get a receipt. And mail it back to me."

I wanted to get mad at him for trying to take charge, and for demanding proof that I did the right thing with his money, but I was too busy trying to swallow the lump in my throat. Which wasn't easy. Not because the lump was so huge, but because the resentment, relief, and the load of other feelings weren't just in my throat, but teeming throughout my entire body.

I walked back toward the entry hall, managing a goodbye wave at the two-year-old menace. She glanced over, her hair dark and glossy like Caffeine's, her blue eyes dulled by the TV, and for an instant she actually looked cute.

Dad followed, hot on my heels. "Nicki? I really hope you didn't mean what you said earlier, that you think I care more about Autumn than you. What I feel is exactly the same. You're both my daughters, even if I live with her."

Everything inside me tightened. I knew then why he'd given me the money. Not because of Mom or me or the possibility of us becoming destitute. Because I'd rubbed his nose in his bias—I'd made him acknowledge out loud that he played favorites.

But I'd gotten what I wanted, so I was willing to be nice.

"Okay, Dad," I managed. "Sure." I peeked out of

the rectangular window beside his door and saw Jared's car.

"I—I've got to go."

"Call me. Tell me how this works out." He squeezed my arm and looked into my eyes. For a second I thought he was going to tell me he loved me. Then he let me go. "And drive carefully."

I can't remember the walk from the house to the car, but suddenly there I was on the curb, reaching for the door handle. The door popped open as if on its own, Jared inside, stretching over the gearshift.

I slid in, touched by his unexpected chivalry. I looked at him to say thanks, and something puppy-dog warm in his eyes gazed back at me. Implying . . . I don't know . . . that he cared about how it had all gone?

And how did I reward this? I burst into tears.

Omigod.

I turned away. Only to feel his hand gently stroke my hair. I wanted to *lurch* away. I mean, this was Jared. The guy who wouldn't talk to me in front of anyone at school. Who made me *pay* him to drive me around.

I was crying. In his car. And he was doing exactly what I was scared of. He was pitying me.

For the rest of the school year, whether on the bleachers or in the halls, whether I was pretending to see him or not—I'd know he'd seen me like this.

Ugh. Suddenly, losing the house and being forced to move didn't seem so bad.

By the time I pulled myself together, we were merging into a sea of red brake lights. Serious freeway traffic. But that was okay. I needed time to decompress before my face-to-face with Mom.

"So what's the story with that?" Jared asked, pointing at my left hand.

For a crazy moment I thought he was asking about my amethyst birthstone ring. It was a gift from my parents on my twelfth birthday—the last we all spent together—and I had this weird habit of twisting it when I was bored, angry, or nevous. Then I saw I was still holding Dad's check.

I folded the check in half and tucked it into my pocket. "Oh—I need to deposit it. On Friday." My thoughts scrambled. "But I can't get out of practice twice in one week, so I don't suppose you could run me to the bank during lunch?"

He threw a look in his rearview mirror, then at me. "My lunch hour fee is double."

For real?

"But," he said, disrupting my disbelief, "I'll settle for a Whopper, fries, and a drink."

After the crying jag, calmness had crept through my body, making me oddly comfortable sitting there in the car. Relaxed, almost. A relieved laugh bubbled inside me, but for some reason I couldn't let it out. Or him off so easily.

"Yeah, Jared, but everybody at school goes to Burger King. We could be seen. The Extra-Hot Senior," I said, making little quotation marks with my bent fingers, "and his little sister's friend. Think of the gossip."

A confident smile blazed across his mouth, which

not only touched his eyes, but strangely touched something in me, too. I didn't know what exactly—and I didn't know if I liked it, either. But the guy was not without style, whether I wanted to admit it or not.

He threw me a look. "Among other things, I'm thinking it will piss Rascal off."

"Rascal?"

"Yeah. After yesterday at your locker, he thinks we're getting together. And it's bugging him."

I felt my jaw drop. "He *told* you that?"

"He didn't have to. It's all over his stupid face."

"So . . . you think he's jealous?" I held myself in check while the "Hallelujah Chorus" played in my head.

"What did I just say?" He turned and glared at me. "Oh, come on, you don't actually still *like* him, do you?"

(Did the joyful notes reflect in my eyes?) "No. No, of course not."

"I mean," his voice noticeably raised, "not after what he did to you?"

I gave my head a firm shake.

"Good. Otherwise you could *walk* home."

I nodded, my thoughts all over the jealous thing. Maybe that was why Kylie had scowled at me during morning break. Maybe she was feeling the vibes he sent out. Maybe—

"So," Jared said, rudely changing the subject. "Are you going to fill me in on the check and the bank deposit, or what?"

Check. Bank. Ugh.

Couldn't we talk more about Rascal being jealous?

But as much as I didn't want to tell him, I figured Jared deserved some kind of explanation for being forced to drive to Ventura. Even if he *was* getting paid for it. So I spilled.

"My mom hasn't closed on a house in months," I blurted out. "She hasn't made any commissions. And it turns out she's fallen behind on the mortgage."

There—I'd said it. I snuck a look his way. Nope, no arrogant smirk. In fact, his brow was heavy, as if in deep thought.

"So she sent you to your dad for money?"

"No, no!" I slipped my ring back and forth over my knuckle. "She'd *kill* me if she knew. That's why all this is top secret. I'm going to make the payment first, then tell her I paid it with the last of my inheritance money from my grandmother."

"Which actually went to . . ."

"Oh, clothes and volleyball shoes and movies," I said, leaving out the chunks I'd dropped on hairdressers who'd promised to make my hair straight and silky. "The rest to the prom dress. And to you."

"Why didn't you return the dress and get your money back?"

"Final sale," I said automatically.

"At a vintage clothing store? Aren't they all about resales?"

Smart boy. The truth was, once I'd zipped myself inside its silkiness, had watched in the mirror as my boyish figure transformed into the body I'd always dreamed of . . . well, there was no going back. Date or no date. Returnable or not. That baby was *mine*.

"Yeah, well," I said, "I just like it, okay?"

He nodded, as if he'd fully processed the data. Then shrugged. "Sorry about your mom. I'd hate to see her lose the house, for you guys to have to move somewhere."

"Thanks," I said, a little flattered, and a little embarrassed, too. My heart sped up, almost in sync with the rhythmical ka-thump of our wheels rolling over the uneven seams in the pavement.

"I mean," he said, "if Alison didn't have *you* to whine to all the time, she'd turn on me. And then I'd have no choice but to grab early admission at any college that would take me and get the hell out of here."

He laughed, and I joined in. Not because what he'd said was particularly funny, but because I wanted to stop feeling miserable. Or at least to pretend.

"But before you try to put one over on your mother, do yourself a favor, and think it all through." He shot me a serious look. "Don't do anything stupid."

Ah, yes. And there was Jared—my big brother.

Live a Little

Sitting in geometry the next morning, I made a startling discovery about my life. About life in general. (Besides the obvious that learning geometry was a waste of perfectly good brain cells.)

I decided that life was like that Chutes and Ladders game you played when you were little. You spin the wheel and move your Mini-Me in a slow and steady progress toward Ultimate Happiness. Unless you land on a ladder that sends you racing to new heights. Or on a slide that tumbles you down, down, down . . .

It seemed that for nine days last June, I was close to

the finish line. Then came the News that sent The Dress to the Back of the Door. My butt had hit that super-long slide, the one that ran almost the full length of the board. And now here I sat, a million miles from victory.

Overly dramatic? Probably. But with the echoes of Dad's voice, my sobbing, and Jared's warning still ringing from last night in my ears, it was getting increasingly hard to have a glass-is-half-full attitude.

Plus, Kylie—whose cinnamon-apple body spray managed to choke me, even though she sat two rows behind and one over—had given me another dirty look this morning. I mean, eye to eye, with a very clear *Die, Loser* written all over it.

When the end-of-class bell finally rang, I followed the throng through the door. A sixth sense told me to scan the hallway crowd, and yep, there was Rascal, leaning against a wall.

Knowing Kylie was just a few designer-shoe steps behind, and not wanting to give her any more ammunition, I acknowledged his nod with a mere lift of my brow. Why tempt fate?

But he took things a bit further. "You and Mc-Creary, huh?" he said as I passed, his steely blue gaze bearing down on me. "What's with that?"

I bit back a grin and managed a monotone response. "Just friends."

"Yeah, right." He grunted as I kept walking. "Hey, Nicolette . . ."

His voice was like a lasso, circling me and pulling me back. But I kept up my pace, moving away—fast. Before my face was taken over by a disfiguring and revealing smile.

Moments later, I was successfully standing beside Alison at her locker.

"You'll be proud of me," I announced.

One side of her mouth curled up. "You managed to sell a property for your mother?"

"Not *that* proud."

"You . . . you . . . got tickets to the Lakers' season opener?"

I gave her a thumbs-down, meaning her next guess should be lower.

"You aced your geometry test?"

"*More*. It's better than that. Last chance."

She shut her locker with a click. "Prouder than acing a test? Um . . . my brother offered you another ride somewhere and you told him where to shove it?"

Her response was so out of left field that it made my head spin. Her message, however, was crystal clear, that she wasn't thrilled with me hanging out with her brother.

Well, neither was I, so no harm, no foul.

"You lose," I said.

"Okay . . ."

"Rascal was outside my class and he tried to talk to me. But I kept on walking." I held her gaze, stubbornly, weakly. "Aren't you proud?"

"I am," she said, and we fell into step together. "Any progress you make toward realizing he's the King of the Losers gets applause from me."

Okay, so why didn't this feel like a compliment?

●

School buzzed by as my mind turned over all the new data it had collected in the past few days. At the end of classes, I made a mad dash for the locker room. There was no way I could be late for practice today.

Zoe was already there, suiting up. The baggy uniform actually flattered her long body, making her legs look like they went on forever. But I liked her anyway.

"What happened to you yesterday?" she asked, glancing up, dark hair framing her heart-shaped face. "I saw you in the hall, but not at practice."

Not showing up for practice at Hillside was *big* news in any sport. We were Division A and the administration was determined to keep every gold cup we had in the gym exactly where it was.

"Luther let me skip—I was sick," I answered simply, and spun the dial on my locker.

She nudged me with a sneakered foot and waited until I looked over. "Was it about a guy?" she asked in a low voice.

"Huh? Why?"

"I pulled the sick thing once," she whispered. "So I could go be with Matt."

Matt was her boyfriend, and of course now I

had my answer as to whether she'd faked or not. But that left me in an awkward position, whether or not to come clean.

The thing was, for a casual friend, Zoe was pretty cool. And she'd told me things that she really shouldn't have, so my conscience made the decision for me. "I went to see my dad," I whispered back.

"Oh," she said quietly, nodding. "Yeah, Luther would have never gone for that."

I touched her arm. "You won't say anything?"

She stood up and started toward the gym, then looked back and gave me an are-you-crazy look. "Hey, I'm guilty, too."

With a sigh of relief, I followed her out of the locker room and caught up with her to start our warm up laps.

Running side by side took effort because her legs were twice as long as mine. But about a year ago, we'd discovered we liked jogging together. We laughed and rolled our eyes at the same kinds of things.

Not to mention that Zoe had become my personal search engine on all things Rascal and Kylie. She was quite the expert, having once brought up the rear of Kylie's Pretty Parade.

She's the one who told me how Kylie and her mom had had a major falling-out during Kylie's parents' divorce. But how Kylie and her mother had mended fences last spring, so Kylie had decided to give living in Phoenix a try. That Kylie had actually *liked* the weeks she'd spent with her mom, until Rascal got tired of being a long-distance boyfriend and asked "another girl" to his junior prom.

Apparently, the two then burned up the phone and Internet lines over me. Until Kylie agreed to come home. Taking Rascal, the love of my miserable life, off the market again. Just like one of the prime real estate properties Mom always talked about, that she couldn't seem to get her hands on.

Like mother, like daughter.

"Okay," Luther said, blowing her whistle. "Positions, everybody. Playtime is *over.*"

If You Give a Girl a Cookie

My heeled sandals apparently went on strike that next morning, because no matter how many piles of clothing I overturned, they remained a no-show.

Flip-flops were my next choice. I could never quite figure out what I hated more—their rhythmic slapping against my heel or the fact that they kept me so low to the ground that I felt like a dwarf.

In any case, I flapped my way to school at my usual hour, through the building, to my locker, and pulled the door open. I gazed into my propped-up mirror to see if my mascara was still on my lashes instead of my skin, and that was when I saw the strange blue paper wedge on top of my geometry book. Probably slipped in through the air vent.

I unfolded the triangle's many sides.

> *Nicolette,*
> *Meet me in the caf*
> *10:05 SHARP!*
> *Your Secret Admirer*

Say *what*?

I twirled around, my head rotating like that girl from *The Exorcist* to see if anyone was watching me—laughing at me—or (dare I wish) looking hopeful.

Nothing.

But come on . . . *secret admirer*? For real?

As I sat in class later, my mind was a whirlwind of nonacademic activity. Of course I knew I should ignore the note, write it off as a prank. Wasn't it the oldest trick in the book? Anybody who liked me or wanted to talk to me would come forward on his own, right?

Unless he was scared. And felt insecure. Kind of like I felt with Rascal. In which case, shouldn't I go and be as kind to the guy as possible, in some sort of cosmic trade-off?

Though I couldn't help thinking about the odds that I'd end up with a dweeb, who I'd have to let down gently.

So why, as the clock struck ten, did I move to the back of the class and pick up the wooden hall pass?

With my heart thumping in time with my flip-flops, I made my way into the caf, only to meet a cavernous room filled with empty lunch tables, some hairnetted ladies, and a curious warm, buttery scent.

"Can I help you?" one of the women asked, shaking her head at me. (Even the new students knew the caf didn't open until eleven-thirty.)

"I—"

"She's with me," spoke a deep and very familiar voice from behind me.

Whoa. I turned.

Rascal. Rascal!

"You?" I managed. "*You* left that note?"

"Had to get you down here somehow. To give you your once-in-a-lifetime experience."

He cupped his hand on my elbow and steered me toward the kitchen. (We were *touching*!)

"Janet," he said. "Joanne. You don't mind if I bring my friend Nicolette back here, do you?"

The ladies smiled shyly, as if they, too, were charmed by him.

He led me to a counter bearing a two-foot aluminum tray, filled with evenly spaced, freshly baked chocolate-chip cookies.

"Straight from the oven. Just wait." He picked up a nearby spatula and scooped up a cookie. Then motioned for me to open my hand, and deposited it.

Warm. Soft.

I took a bite. The chocolate goo'd and stretched.

Heaven.

"Good, huh?" he said, and crammed an entire cookie into his mouth.

I watched him chomp. Then he leaned in. So close I could see a tiny smear of chocolate on the corner of his mouth. His voice went kinda sexy. "There's only one thing I can think of that's better."

I swallowed my bite (proud that I didn't choke), thanked the ladies, and turned to head toward the door without answering him. And I made it to the door without saying a word, Rascal following.

But when I got to the door, I stopped and turned back. I was confused by more than one thing, but all I could manage to say was "How did you pull this off? You know—get special treatment in the caf?" I mean, when I'd worked in the middle school caf, the only person I remembered getting anything for free was Kylie, and that was chicken soup. And that was because she'd been sick.

He gave me an innocent smile and answered easily. "Sometimes the coach calls us in for early-morning practices. Afterward, we're all starving, so me and some of the guys come down here, offer to take out trash or move boxes or whatever in exchange for food. One day, Janet mentioned the cookies at ten o'clock. Ever since, I've been dropping by."

I eyed him evenly. "Don't you ever go to class?"

"Sure. When I feel like it."

He winked at me, and I knew there was no way I

was seeing something that wasn't there. He was flirting. But why? What was going on?

Confused, yet unmistakably happy, I pushed open the caf door and, as if on autopilot, floated back to my classroom. Maybe Rascal was sweeter than everyone gave him credit for?

I knew better than to tell Alison about the cookie escapade. She'd only scold me for falling for another of Rascal's stunts, remind me I was setting myself up to get hurt. Again. And that he was still Kylie's boyfriend.

All things I totally knew, deep down.

Instead, when I met up with her later, I asked if she wanted to go with Jared and me to the bank. I didn't want her getting any wrong ideas about her brother giving me rides. And besides, why should I have to endure more uncomfortable alone time with him? But when I asked, she shook her head, saying she was reading a great romance novel.

That sounded better to me, too. But it didn't keep me from begging. "It'll be fun."

"Fun?"

"Okay, maybe not *fun*, but . . ."

She held up her hand. "I get it. And thanks for asking me this time."

This time? What? Had she wanted to go up to my dad's? But I didn't get to dwell on it. A deep guy-voice, speaking my name, interrupted us and Alison and I turned to see Jared's friend Mitch. He was tall, thin, with an upturned nose that gave shorties like me a view straight into his brain. *Nice.*

"I was thinking," he said, aiming this goofy expression at me, "that I might need help with the Spanish test next week. I might need to call you."

I was confused. Was my C+ something he envied?

"So why don't you give me your phone number?" he went on.

To shut him up and move him along, Alison rattled it off. He scribbled it down, then ripped off a corner of a page, wrote his own phone number, and passed it to me. To be polite, I accepted it, but knew I'd never dial it.

The next thing I knew, Jared sauntered up; then, after a few words, Alison made her excuses and it was just Jared and me, heading for the front door.

Looking everywhere but at each other.

I had been hoping that maybe we'd actually gotten past the awkwardness, but when I'd passed him earlier at the Senior Bench, he'd looked right through me. Now we were hardly talking.

Old habits die hard, I guess.

When we stepped outside, the hot sun blasted us. He slipped on a pair of dark shades and started walking in the direction of the north gate. I moved closer to him, simply because the outdoor lunch area was crowded. We passed groups of kids from several different cliques, but it didn't take a rocket scientist to see that Jared was the one getting the nods and hellos.

"You need to be back for fifth period?" he asked as we hit the side street.

"Yeah," I answered, wondering if it was a coincidence that he chose until we left campus to finally speak to me.

"Doesn't give us much time."

I struggled to set my mind back to business. "We don't need much. I just need to fill out a form and hand over the check."

"And we've got to eat."

My stomach was in a knot from all the morning's action—I couldn't imagine eating. "Maybe *you* do."

He shot me a look, but with his eyes behind sunglasses, I had to go to his mouth and cheeks for a true reading of his thoughts. "At some point, Nic, I need food. Growing guy and all. Plus, I go straight from school today to my uncle's print shop. *And* it's part of the deal."

Yeah, yeah.

Approaching the rear of his Camaro, we split to our respective sides.

"So," he called over the top of the car. "Burger King before or after?"

"After."

He slipped inside and popped open the passenger-door lock. Then sat back and turned the key in the ignition.

I opened the door and climbed in. Carefully—the seat was hot against my mostly bare legs. I don't know if it was the sizzling vinyl or maybe the same nerves that wrenched my belly, but I snapped at him. "You could do with some seat covers. And what, you're only gentlemanly enough to open the door for me at night?"

"I only opened the door for you because you were crying."

"I wasn't crying!" Not *then*.

"You were about to."

"How did you know that?"

Jared shrugged. "You wouldn't have asked me to drive you if it wasn't really important. And you seemed nervous in the car, and then uncomfortable around him.

"*And* he reminds me a little of my dad," he said, and slowed for a red light. "Has his own agenda. Fathers like that can do a number on their kids. Make the girls cry, the guys punch holes in walls."

"You've punched holes in the wall?"

"Once or twice. But mostly I just try to keep the peace." He turned, and despite his dark glasses, I could tell he was looking straight into me. "I have a feeling you do, too."

I laughed sarcastically. "Yeah, by keeping our phone calls and visits to the bare minimum."

"For me, it's woodworking. Sometimes I can't wait to get to school and get my hands on the table saw."

I wrinkled my brow. "You really like it that much?"

"Hey, don't knock it till you've tried it."

I guess I couldn't argue with that.

The line between the red ropes at the bank was blessedly short, but at the window the teller pointed us to a desk on the other side of the room. Tension knotted in my neck, and my stomach was about as serene as the evening sky on July 4. Several desks filled a carpeted platform. A lady with collagen "trout" lips sat behind a plaque calling her an account manager. Jared and I walked over, and after quietly explaining that we wanted to make a payment, sat down across from her.

"Why isn't your parent handling this?" she asked, eyeing me over half-glasses.

"My dad *is* handling this," I insisted, my voice cracking. "See, that's his signature on the check. And it's made out to the bank. I'm just dropping it off."

Her brow arched. "What I don't understand is why this payment isn't being made through our payment center, or by one of the mortgagees on the account."

Jared, who sat in a cushioned chair beside me, leaned forward. "Her parents are busy. You see," he said, and dropped his voice to just above a whisper, "they've gotten a little behind financially. And Nicolette here is trying to do her part to get the family back on track."

The woman's face softened. "And you, young man? What is your role in this?"

"I'm her driver."

I didn't know if it was Jared's gentle tone, or the fact

67

that he'd taken off his sunglasses and played up his root beer–colored eyes. But the lines in the lady's forehead faded like they'd been shot with Botox, and she reached for her receipt pad.

"Well, nice to see such enterprising young people."

"No slackers here," he said, exaggerating his smile.

Not that I didn't appreciate his efforts, but it was everything I could do to keep a straight face for the rest of the transaction. Which, barring the initial questioning, went faster than I'd thought it would.

Back at the car, we settled in and buckled our seat belts. Jared jutted his chin out. "That went well, huh?"

"Yeah." I turned toward him. "Though it wouldn't have if you hadn't flirted with that lady."

"That wasn't flirting."

"That *so* was flirting!"

"This," he said, and let the corners of his mouth tug into a smile that touched off a sparkle in his eyes, "is flirting."

I tried to laugh—I mean, come on, this coming from a guy who basically put up with me for an hourly fee—but his smile set off something smack-dab in the middle of my chest, and my laugh came out more like a strangled gasp. What was going on?

Persistent to prove his point (or maybe egged on by my confused reaction?), he trailed a finger down my cheek, then tucked some strands of hair behind my ear.

I wanted to give him a shove. This was *Jared*. It was just too creepy. But I didn't do a thing. I just sat there, mute and paralyzed. Until he pulled his hand away.

"The thing in the bank," he said, his face relaxing, "was called negotiating. Telling the lady what she wanted so we could get what we wanted."

His words jump-started my brain. A memory formed, a certain business teacher discussing *The Art of the Deal*. And I was more than happy to change the course of the conversation. "I take it you took Intro to Business in tenth grade, too?"

"Yeah. I thought it was all crap at the time, but now that I'm writing college apps and working for my uncle, some of it is starting to come in handy."

Negotiation skills helped me, too. With my parents. The coach. Even Jared. (Nice to know that some of the junk they taught us in school had a purpose.)

I watched him flip his visor, grab hold of his sunglasses, and slip them back over his eyes.

"We're outta here," he said, "and with time to spare. I think you should be thanking me."

"Oh, you do, do you?"

"Totally. What would you do without me, Nic?"

"I'd get by, I think," I said, biting back a grin.

His tone went flip. "Don't mention it."

I lifted my hand to give him a playful punch. Like I had the other day. Then dropped it back in my lap. Because I realized—not that I had a crush on him or anything—that touching Jared was nice. Too nice.

●

Minutes later, Jared was turning into the BK driveway. But instead of continuing to the drive-thru, he parked and got out.

As we headed up the walkway, he fell into step beside me.

"We have time to eat inside. You *are* going to eat something, right? You're not one of those idiot girls who doesn't eat in front of a guy?"

With the mortgage paid, I did feel a little hungry. But Jared wasn't getting off that easy. "Actually, I am. I totally freak out around cute guys. But at the moment, I'm hungry enough to eat a horse."

He shot me a dirty look, and I smiled back.

Things were returning to normal. I could finally take a breath and relax. Or so I thought.

When we actually entered Burger King to see Rascal and about five of his friends occupying a front booth, I knew my troubles weren't over at all.

Crap. A coincidence? Maybe. All those people had seen us leave together. But this *was* the only fast-food place within walking distance of school.

Six pairs of eyes turned on us. Their voices silenced.

I would have *loved* to have taken credit—to believe the shimmering tension was all about me. But the eye daggers Rascal and Jared were throwing at each other had entirely too much depth, too much history.

"McCreary," spat Rascal.

"Rascal," replied Jared, with venom.

Both guys were seeing red and practically scraping their hooves for a fight.

Top Ten Uses for an Unworn Prom Dress

#8

**Push between two idiots and crack The Dress
like a matador's cape—even though two cows do not
make a bull, the BS is sure to start flying.**

What was this about? Had Jared messed with Kylie at some point?

Nah. Alison would have mentioned it.

A smile must have taken over my face, because suddenly Jared turned his iron gaze on me, then made a hard turn into the line to order.

I followed.

"What are you so happy about?" he snapped. "Did you know he was going to be here?"

"No," I mumbled with more frown than voice. "You're the one who suggested this place."

His jaw clenched as if he wanted to say something,

then decided to keep it inside. "Okay. What do you want?"

"A cheeseburger. Diet Coke." I went for the ten in my front pocket.

His hand stopped mine in midair, touching me for just an instant. A nice instant. A really confusing instant. "It's on me."

"But you said—"

"I'm paying, Nic."

He retrieved his wallet from his back pocket, and I swear he threw a look over his shoulder at Rascal, as well. A look that said: *She's with me*.

Okay, so while I got that this weirdness had nothing to do with me, I was also pretty sure Jared was using me to his advantage. Which meant I had a right to know what this was all about.

And hey, I'd fessed up about my mother and the mortgage, so fair was fair.

He told the cashier we wanted the food to go, paid, and grabbed the paper sack. I grabbed the cups, filled up the drinks, and followed him toward the exit.

My heart went into a giddyup as we approached Rascal and his friends. Rascal, now outside the booth, was lounging with his backside against the table. His feet could easily reach out and trip a passerby. If he wanted them to.

Did he dare? Would World War III break out here in the restaurant?

Just stay cool, I said in my head.

Or at least I *thought* it was in my head. But suddenly my words were hanging in the air. And Rascal, whose gaze I was holding, was shrugging.

"I *am* cool, Nicolette. I'm the coolest guy you'll ever know."

I could feel Jared's muscles tighten beside me. *So* not good.

"Well," I said, thinking fast on my unsteady feet, "that makes you and Jared exact opposites, then."

All eyes moved to me like I was the center of a french fry–smelling universe. The Burger Queen.

"Yeah, Rascal," I said, my thoughts racing, "you're definitely the coolest guy I know. But Jared?" I said, forcing a smug smile. "He's the hottest."

Silence. Except for a lady and some kids at another booth who didn't seem to understand the dire necessity of defusing this situation.

Then one of Rascal's friends chuckled. Damon or Harrison or someone. Then another. Then Rascal himself.

I couldn't even *think* of looking over at Jared. Who might like the fact that I'd called him hot. But also, might not.

Rascal's mouth bunched into an all-knowing smile. "I think you're going to change your mind about which one of us is hottest, Nicolette. Sooner, if not later."

I swallowed—hard. Was he implying there'd be an "us"—a Rascal and me—in the future?

Jared took a long, hard stride forward. "I'm more

than happy to take Kylie into my backseat and let her be the final judge of who's hot and who's not," he spat at Rascal.

Okay . . . not so good anymore. Besides the fact that the level of testosterone had me gasping like an asthmatic, I knew I had to get Jared out of Burger King before something bad happened.

I grabbed his hand, and to my shock, he didn't fight my grasp. In fact, he laced his fingers through mine.

Rascal's eyes took on a death-ray-like glare. "Kylie's off-limits."

"Yeah?" Jared said. "Well, so is Nicolette."

I was?

I was!

The room went spinning. As much as I wanted this to last forever and ever and ever, I knew this was dangerous territory.

"Come on, Jared," I said, in a fake girly whine. "We've got to get back to school."

The guys glared at each other, and then Jared turned, all red-faced, and walked out with me.

He didn't drop my hand until we reached the passenger door of his car, when he used his key to turn the lock for me.

Moments later, we were zooming out of the lot.

"So I—I'm off-limits?" I stammered over the blast from the air-conditioning vents.

"To him, anyway. He's got a girlfriend. And you're too smart to let him sniff around you again."

Huh. I was a little disappointed. Although I wasn't sure why. His answer was so logical.

"And I didn't need your help in there, Nic," he continued, squinting at the windshield, so obviously preoccupied and ticked off that he'd forgotten to put his shades back on. "I can fight my own battles."

"I know that. But you stepped up for me at the bank," I defended myself lamely.

He ground his teeth. "That was different."

"Yeah, but somehow I'm involved in this, so I deserve to know what's happening." I pulled the wrapper off a straw and plunked it into my Diet Coke. "Is this about . . . her? Did you go out with her at some point?" (For some reason, I couldn't bring myself to say Kylie's name.)

"I've never touched Kylie."

"Did something happen at school?"

"We're not even in the same classes."

Oh, yeah, Jared was all AP. And Rascal . . . well, he was known more for his feats on the football field and in the hallways.

Jared grabbed his burger, took a bite, and swallowed, ignoring me. Then, finally, he broke. "The fact is I hate him as much as he hates me. And since I've been driving you around again, and you seem to be the only girl at school who doesn't quiver in his presence, it's making him crazy."

He veered around a car, then looked at me, his voice losing its hard edge. "Okay, I guess I should thank you.

You kind of kept me in check back there. Especially taking my hand like that. It distracted me."

I reached for the air-conditioning vent and tilted it toward me, suddenly all kinda warm. "You're welcome."

"And from here on, I'll keep you out of it. You've got enough on your mind."

I took a bite of my burger before my thoughts fell out of my mouth again and got me in real trouble. If I'm not mistaken, I think I kind of liked being in the thick of this thing.

●

When I stumbled in from practice, Mom was soaking in the tub.

"There's a chicken Caesar in the fridge!" she called through the slightly open bathroom door. "Help yourself!"

I was starving, but before I could eat I needed a short pit stop. It was silly and flat-out embarrassing, but I really, really wanted time with The Dress.

Needed it.

I'd done the shower thing in the locker room, so I didn't have to worry about sweat or anything unseemly defacing its perfection.

I unzipped the bag and inhaled the fabric's sweetness. I could swear the soft rose color and the tiny embroidered flower buds gave off a scent all their own. I shed my shorts and tee, zipped myself inside its elegance, and turned to gaze in the mirror. The waistline somehow gave me an hourglass shape, and the color looked rich against my fading summer tan. But most of all, the pure enchantment of The Dress showed in my eyes. They were almost gleaming.

I moved to the bed, turned, and did one of those trust falls. Hard enough to set the springs of the bed screaming, but hyperaware not to harm the fabric or stitching on The Dress, of course.

A single ring from the cordless phone broke my musing. Mindlessly, I reached for it and pressed ON. And heard a male voice.

"Hey, Nic."

Rascal?

Jared?

Fire lit my face.

"Hey," I managed, sitting up, telling myself to get a grip.

"Something I wanted to talk about," he said.

The voice sounded deep, like Jared. Besides, why would Rascal call me? There was no date to break.

"Something I thought about after we went to class."

Class. Oh, *definitely* Jared.

"You doing anything tomorrow?" he continued.

"Not really," I said, thanking God there wasn't widespread use of video phones yet. How would I explain to Jared —how would I explain to *anyone*—why I was sitting in a pink crinoline gown at six o'clock on a Friday evening? Alone?

"Good," he said. "I'll pick you up at around noon, all right?"

"Okay, Jared," I said, just to be sure.

"Bring one of your mother's business cards. And a picture of her."

"Huh?"

"I'll explain tomorrow." He paused and sort of laughed. "And it'll give you something to think about."

I didn't need anything to think about. My brain was already overloaded. What I needed was to get *off* the phone and *out* of this dress.

"So, yeah, tomorrow," I said, looking down at myself, caught in a weird net of fantasy and reality. "Okay, see you then." I hung up and shuffled toward the hanger on the back of my door, and with a hot face and a funny feeling in the pit of my stomach, retired The Dress to its home.

All the Blues That's Fit to Print

The next morning, I did my usual Saturday sleep-in and long, lazy shower. Then I broke with tradition. I reached under the sink for the blow-dryer. Luckily, Mom was sitting an open house for some other realtor or I would have gotten Twenty Questions from her. She'd grill me about boys, ask me who I was trying to impress.

Ugh.

Anyway, I *hated* blow-drying my hair. Not only did my arm get achy, but no matter what I did, my hair never looked any better. Tight blond curls turned to yellow frizz. But for some reason, that morning, I felt like breaking new ground. I told myself if I only tried *hard* enough . . . But after a good forty-five minutes, no luck. I got the totally predicted result.

I did my thing with a palmful of gel. Then I dug up my favorite clips, pulled back the loose strands from my face, and went to my closet. No dress code to worry about, so I went with low jean shorts and a peachy crop top. I would have killed for a belly ring.

I topped off my look with some mascara and this really pretty pink lip gloss. You'd almost think I was trying to impress someone. I was only going somewhere with Jared, to do something with my mother's picture and her business card—but you never know, right?

I'm not sure why, but my pulse did a little jump when the white Camaro rounded the corner. I locked the front door and moved to the edge of the curb. Only to see a silhouette in the seat beside him.

Several inches shorter than Jared. With longish hair. A girl.

A girl?

He'd never mentioned anything about a girl. A girl friend. Or girlfriend. Alison had never said anything—

Of course. Alison.

God, was I an idiot, or what?

My best friend's face came into view as Jared rolled to a stop. She pushed the door open and leaned forward so I could crawl into the back.

"Hey, Nic," she said, and smiled.

I felt relieved. Foolish. Embarrassed. But when Alison swiveled around to take in my look, embarrassment won hands down.

"I like what you did with your hair," she said, and slammed the door.

I shrugged. "I was bored this morning."

"You should be bored more often. Seriously."

"Thanks. Hey, I didn't know you were coming today," I said, hoping to sidetrack the conversation away from why I'd picked this morning, of all mornings, to spiff up. Then realized my comment was exactly the wrong thing to say. It probably seemed like I wanted to spend time alone with her brother.

"Her idea," Jared said, eyeing me in the rearview mirror.

"Well, someone has to keep Nic company at the mall."

"I told you," he said. "Mom could have dropped you off *later*, after we were done."

"Okay! I either need a translator," I said, "or someone's gotta start speaking my language."

"We're going to the print shop," Jared said. Our gazes connected in the mirror. No sunglasses this time. Just dark eyes, looking slightly amused.

"My uncle's got tons of extra paper lying around. I thought we'd make some promotional stuff for your mother. Flyers. Notepads. Things she could hand out so people get to know her name."

"Wow. Great. But how much is this going to cost?"

"*Nada*. My uncle said we could use the paper for free," he went on. "And he'd overlook the toner charges as long as we don't go crazy."

"The thing is," Alison said, turning around, her green gaze brightening, "at around two o'clock, some rush-rush project is coming in, and Jared's gotta help. So you and I can bum around Fashion Square till he's done."

"Cool," I said, because it was. Though I felt kinda weird leaving Jared to do all the work, and kinda curious and thankful that he'd go out of his way to help me at all—shouldn't I maybe stay with him and offer to help?

But something told me to keep my mouth shut. That giving off the impression that I preferred to be with Jared—even just out of gratitude—wouldn't sit well with Alison.

Or maybe Jared, either?

●

Their uncle's shop was in the back of a minimall just a couple of blocks from the sprawling Fashion Square—where everybody in and around our school chose to shop.

Jared fired up the computer and found a layout program while Alison scanned in my mom's picture and her logo. On top he typed "EVERYTHING I TOUCH . . . TURNS TO *SOLD*!" which he said he'd dreamed up while bored in class. My contribution was a line across the bottom calling Mom "Thurman Oaks' Top-Selling Realtor," which we all agreed had a real ring to it. Then we printed it out on eye-catching neon-pink paper.

By the time their uncle came in with the do-or-die project, we'd printed a huge stack of flyers—like five hundred or something.

Now, if *that* didn't generate some business for Mom, what would? I couldn't wait to show them to her.

Alison and I headed out the door, although leaving Jared to do all the work tugged at me like the last bit of Chunky Monkey in the freezer. But he didn't seem to mind, just said he'd call Alison on her cell phone when he was done.

Soon we were pushing through the doors of Macy's, and Alison, whose parents were the opposite of mine— meaning rich—was stopping to admire an adorable purse with outside compartments and a designer name etched into its leather.

"I love it," she said, and hiked the straps over her shoulder. "But it's so small. I don't think you can get a wallet and cell phone inside at the same time."

"That's because the kind of person who can afford it brings a servant along to hold her things."

We laughed as she put the purse back on the rack.

That's when we saw them. Cherry and Natalia, two of Kylie's chief hangers-on. Sitting on high swivel seats at the makeup counter, applying blush and glaring at us.

Or was it just at *me*? If I'd been reading the squinty

eyes of their fair leader correctly, Kylie had recently upgraded me from totally insignificant to number one on her hit list.

I looked right past them.

"Don't look now . . . ," Alison said, in a small voice under a big, fake smile.

"Yeah, Pretty Parade alert," I said, covering my mouth with a nose scratch.

"Seriously." She picked up another purse, a hideous royal blue thing, and held it up, just below her eyes. "Think that means Kylie's nearby?"

I turned my back to the girls. "Only if this is the worst day of my life."

"And you already had *that* day, right? When you had to see your dad."

Actually, Jared had done the proverbial "make lemonade out of lemons" thing with that day for me. But this was *not* the time to say that.

"It's safe to say," I responded instead, "that every day with my dad is a new low."

Alison laughed, too loudly, to show Cherry and Natalia we were *not* interested in their presence or intimidated. She put the purse down and glanced their way. "Cherry's on her phone now, talking furiously."

"Calling their queen, probably." I searched Alison's face. "What's our game plan? Stay here? Go to Bloomie's?"

She shrugged. "We go about our business as if we didn't see them. I don't know about you, but I could really go for an Ice Blended Mocha right now."

I nodded. Especially since the coffee place was a good thousand footsteps away. Was Alison a friend or what?

Minutes later, we were sucking gobs of frozen coffee and whipped cream through straws, strolling past clothing shops, shoe stores, and places that sold upscale gadgets.

"Omigod, look at that skirt." Alison had stopped dead in her tracks and was pointing to a mannequin in a doorway. "Seriously. Of course, baby pink is *so* not my color, but if they have it in green or blue . . ." She handed me her drink. "Give me a minute, okay?" she said, and rushed past the NO FOOD OR DRINK sign posted beside the store entrance.

After standing in the doorway feeling slightly stupid, I moved to a nearby bench and plopped down. I couldn't help thinking about Jared back at the print shop, and whether we should have stayed to help. But then a voice gave me a swift kick back to reality.

"Uh, hell-*oh*?"

I looked up and into Kylie's hard blue eyes.

Cherry hovered at one side. Natalia closed in on the other.

I waited for my life to flash before me and thought of all the hours I'd wasted practicing volleyball when I could have been perfecting something constructive, something that could have helped me at this very moment. Kickboxing. Karate. Projectile vomiting.

No, wait! Time out!

I was in Fashion Square. On a Saturday afternoon. With moms and dads and kids passing by. And security . . . well, men in uniforms were around somewhere, I was sure. Besides, these three weren't cold-blooded killers. They were just popular.

"Hi," I said, for lack of anything better to say.

When none of them answered, I tried a smile.

Then I tightened my hold on the Ice Blended Mochas.

Just in case.

Hairstyles of the Rich and Popular

"We need to talk," Kylie said, waving for me to make room for her on the mall bench.

She threw looks at her mascaraed bodyguards, who obediently backed off. But I remained on high alert, my hands anchored around the frosty drinks. (Palms losing sensation—but one crisis at a time, if you don't mind.)

"We'll be in A and F if you need us," Cherry said, leading Natalia away.

Kylie sank down, eye level with me. I looked at blond hair so exquisitely streaked that no two strands were the same shade. Perfectly smoky eyeshadow under finely penciled brows. And lip liner etched around a pretty coral gloss.

She probably spent more time on her face every morning than I would have for the prom.

Had I gotten to go.

"Okay, girl to girl," she said, actually meeting my eye. "Let's get this thing ironed out."

I didn't have to be a genius to realize she meant Rascal's sudden, renewed interest in me. It wasn't like she and I had a friendship to fix. Or that we'd spoken since she'd spread those lame rumors about me food-poisoning her.

And actually, it kind of surprised me that she'd go so far as a face-to-face with me about Rascal. I mean, did she really find me threatening? Her boyfriend was just a flirt. And didn't the snitch who told her I was going to be Rascal's prom date give her the 411 on how he'd asked me out of the blue, and how, even then, we'd barely spent any time together?

"Look, Kylie," I said, now resting a mocha on the bench and warming my frozen-tundra palm against my shorts. "There's nothing between Rascal and me. I was just a substitute prom date."

She sniffed, her body arching like her marionette strings had been pulled. "I know that."

"Okay. Well, he and I hardly ever talk. I mean, sure, outside my Spanish class sometimes, but that hardly counts." Then I took a sip of my mocha (or maybe it was Alison's), thinking it was probably a good time to shut up.

She tapped perfect nails on the bench. "I'm here about our boyfriends."

Our . . . *Hello?*

"Rascal and Jared are at each other's throats," she said, and frowned so hard that actual wrinkles creased her forehead. "I'm afraid they're going to throw punches and Rascal will get suspended before the homecoming game. We have to do something."

I just sighed.

First of all, Rascal might be spectacular to watch in those tight pants and padded jerseys, and his performance on the field was good and all—but the football team was undefeated. They could most definitely win without him.

But, more importantly, she'd really gotten things twisted. Jared was too pigheaded to be swayed by anything I had to say. Meanwhile, Rascal had slipped that note into my locker, had been talking and pretty much flirting with me. He'd even kind of offered to fight Jared for me.

Kylie flipped a handful of hair back off her forehead and continued. "I think, as their girlfriends, we should try to find a way to help them burn the hatchet."

"Bury," I choked out.

"What?"

"Bury the hatchet, not burn."

She frowned.

I put down the other mocha. As well as my guard. There was no reason to be nervous about this. "Look, I'd love to help, but I'm not Jared's girlfriend."

Her gaze narrowed. "That's not what people are saying."

People . . . who? People like Keith and Mitch from the Senior Bench? The ones who thought that I was putting out for him to drive me around? Or Rascal and his friends in Burger King? Yeah, real in-the-know people.

"Sorry to break this to you, Kylie, but I know a little more on the topic of my love life."

She seemed to look right through me. "Well, I was thinking if the four of us got together, had pizza or something—"

"No," I said, standing. "No four of us."

"Nicolette," she whined.

"Look, can *you* talk Rascal into this sit-down?"

"I figured we could sort of trick them. Maybe pick a time to meet at the same pizzeria."

"Yeah, well, nothing I can do." Or even wanted to do.

"If you could just talk to Jared . . ."

"I hardly know the guy, okay? He's, you know, my best friend's brother."

Alison emerged from the shop, a cell phone to her ear. "Nic!" she called, then froze for a heartbeat while acknowledging me and my unusual companion. "Uh, Jared's on his way to pick us up!"

I waved in recognition and turned to see Kylie

standing up. She dwarfed me in both height and social stature. "Promise me you'll talk to him."

I twisted my ring.

"*Promise* me, Nicolette. This one thing. When have I ever asked anything of you?"

Something inside me exploded. I wanted to find the mall intercom and respond in front of everyone:

Ask anything of me?

YOU are the reason I missed out on the most astonishing night of my high school life.

Ask anything of me? MUCH?

But staring into her *Hello? Anyone home?* eyes, I bit back those words to give her what she wanted. I had a feeling that making her wish come true might be more fun than denying it. "Well, okay," I said, "I'll ask him."

Smug satisfaction settled on her face. "Great. We'll talk Monday before geometry."

Talk? At school? In front of people? Wow, Chunky sure was anxious for her man to play in the homecoming game.

"Can't wait," I said, going so light on the sarcasm I doubted she'd pick it up.

I caught up with Alison, and soon we were heading across the mall, toward the parking lot, recounting the past few minutes.

"You settle this thing between Jared and Rascal," Alison told me, "and Kylie will be eternally grateful. At least as long as she remembers. She might even invite you to a party at her house or something."

I laughed scornfully. "Now, *that's* my idea of heaven. A whole night of watching the two of them make out!"

Jared was idling at the curb outside Macy's. Sunglasses sat over his eyes, making him look oddly *GQ*-esque.

Alison opened the door and slid into the back. I knew it was only so I could have Jared's full attention about the Kylie thing, but still, I appreciated her giving me the front.

"So, Jared," I said, moving the stack of flyers from the floor to my lap. "I had a heart-to-heart with Kylie in the mall."

"Kylie?"

"Yeah. We ran into her."

"Or it could be Cherry called her when she saw us," Alison piped up.

I gave him a moment to let this sink in, knowing the guy brain didn't have the same ability to process rapid-fire, random information as the girl brain. "Yeah, anyway, she wants you and Rascal to make up so he doesn't get suspended before the homecoming game."

I held my breath.

"Tell Kylie Shoenbacher," Jared said, his hands clenched around the steering wheel, "that she can kiss my ass."

Alison poked her head through the opening of the two seats, and together we burst out laughing.

"I can't wait," I said.

●

Mexican seasonings woke up my senses when I cruised through the front door.

Uh-oh. Mom's enchiladas were to die for. But since Dad had left, she'd only labored over complicated dishes when she was upset.

I plopped the flyers upside down on the coffee table and followed the aroma. "Smells good," I said, instead of hello.

She looked up from a saucepan. "Hi, honey. Where were you?"

"At the mall with Alison."

"Buy anything?"

I shook my head and saw relief flash in her eyes. Slipping into a kitchen chair, I asked about the open house.

"A few Looky Lous. That's all." A huge sigh seemed to rise from deep within her. In a scratchy voice, she continued, "But remember the couple from Nevada? Whose whole office was transferring out here?"

Worry balled in my stomach. I knew she hated being a realtor, but *I* hated the fact that she was failing so miserably at it.

"Yeah?"

"They bought through another realtor." She stirred the enchilada sauce furiously. "I was counting on their commission. And all the future sales from their coworkers, too. I thought things were turning around for me." She blew some loose hairs off her face and then let out a laugh, sad and hollow.

"Mom," I said, feeling a well of emotion in my throat. I had to tell her. It was time. "You can forget about the mortgage for right now. I—I went to the bank and paid the total due."

She turned. "You did . . . what? When?"

"Yesterday. During lunch. Jared drove me."

"Where'd you get the money?"

"The money from Grandma," I said, suddenly focused on the linoleum floor. "I knew you were strapped. And I still had a bunch left over."

"I didn't think you had *that* much. I mean, she only left you . . ." She stared off into space, then back at me. "That was wonderful of you . . . really wonderful. I hate that you spent your own money to keep a roof over our heads. But that was wonderful."

"Don't worry about it."

She suddenly lunged at me and gave me a noisy kiss on my forehead. "You are the most unselfish, loving daughter in the world! And I swear to you—on your grandmother's grave—that I will pay back every penny of that. With interest."

I forced a smile, but I could feel its edges trembling. "I don't want the money back, Mom. Forget it."

"Forget it?" She let out another laugh. One filled with relief. Joy.

That struck my conscience like a devil with a pitchfork.

"Forget it?" she repeated. "Not only will I remember this kindness as long as I live, Nicolette, I may even take an ad out in the newspaper to tell everyone the incredible thing you did for me!"

I faked another smile. She'd better be exaggerating. Or else I had to hope that the newspaper wasn't available as far north as my dad's place.

●

I left Mom in her giddy glory, snatched the flyers, and headed to my room. After closing the door, I slid the stack under a Lakers sweatshirt in my closet. No way I wanted her seeing them now.

I'd paid her bills with money from the man she hated. I'd lied to her face and pretended the money was the very same I'd selfishly pissed away ages ago. And all in the name of helping.

Helping *myself* was more like it.

I flopped down on my bed and was trying to concentrate on the little rocks in the cottage-cheese ceiling when the phone rang.

Alison started talking as soon as I picked up. "Okay, so Jared said something pretty interesting after we dropped you off," she started in immediately. "He doesn't think Kylie really cares about the homecoming game as much as the homecoming *dance*."

I sat up. *Go*, Jared.

"He thinks she's afraid Rascal will be suspended from the game, and then they won't be able to go to the dance, either, disqualifying them from being named king and queen. And since they're seniors, of course, it's now or never."

"Sure," I said, thinking aloud. "What do you bet she's already written her acceptance speech and purchased her royal gown?"

"Or was shopping for it when Cherry and Natalia saw us?"

I hummed in agreement. "All she needs is her tiara."

"And her king to stay out of trouble."

"Tell Jared he's a regular Sherlock Holmes."

She was silent for a beat. "Better I don't. It was just a passing comment. And he already thinks you have some kind of an obsession about dances and dresses."

I felt blood rush to my face.

Well, of course he would, having spent so much time driving me from store to store. Hearing what was wrong with the first gazillion dresses I'd tried on, and *so right* about my one-of-a-kind vintage find. I'd probably babbled like an idiot.

My gaze flew to the back of my door, to the garment bag encasing the loveliest, softest, sweetest dress ever.

Aaaahhhh.

Okay, so maybe I *did* have a bit of an obsession going on. But The Dress was incredible—whether or not I got to wear it outside my room. Besides, there *were* other uses for it. Plenty of uses.

Top Ten Uses for an Unworn Prom Dress

#7

Drape it over your bed, for while you may never be prom queen, at least you'll sleep in princesslike splendor (and avoid mosquito bites).

I shook my head as if to rid myself of my ridiculousness and kept listening to Alison, who was now asking how Mom's open house had gone. Another subject I didn't want to discuss. But these things were apparently out of my control. I shifted gears and gave her the scoop, including how I'd owned up to paying the mortgage.

"Did she ask a million questions, guess where the money came from, and throw things?"

"No, no, just the opposite. She totally believed it was from my bank account and acted like I was the best daughter in the world."

"Ouch."

"Totally." I exhaled, my gaze drifting to the Lakers sweatshirt in the open closet. "So I figure I'd better spend tomorrow passing out the flyers. Secretly, you know, to help her get more business, but without her going all crazy about how totally wonderful I am."

"Yeah," she said, and made a noise like she agreed. "I wish I could help, but my mother's on a rampage about my room. She's 'made time' tomorrow to help me with a complete overhaul. It's going to be one *long* day."

"Well, when we're college roommates, we can have competitions to see whose side of the room can be the messiest."

"Seriously."

A knuckled rap sounded on my door. "Dinner, honey. And I made hot fudge to pour over ice cream for dessert."

God, she knew how to hurt a person.

"I gotta go," I told Alison.

"Wait." She stopped me. "One last thing. Did you hear from Mitch?"

"Mitch?"

"Yeah, about Spanish, or whatever."

"No." I had totally forgotten about that. "And I don't want to," I added. "But hey, if you like him, I could maybe call him and set something up where you're there, too?"

"No thanks," she said, and seemed to laugh.

After I hung up I stood there for a second and took a deep breath, readying myself for my mom. Realizing that asking Jared for the ride and Dad for the money might actually have been the easy part. What might kill me was this—pretending to be worthy of Mom's hot-fudge adoration.

●

I was relieved to wake up the next morning to a note saying a prospective client had called and asked Mom to show him some properties. Not only did it mean the possibility of an eventual paycheck, but it made my day easier. I wouldn't have to smuggle the flyers outside or lie about where I was going.

But for some odd reason, the best part of the morning was when I opened the front door to see my best friend's brother on the step, jangling his car keys.

"I hear you've got a job to do." Jared dug his hand into the pocket of his board shorts.

A smile took over my face. It felt too big, actually. But just being near him again lit a weird, happy glow inside me. "Yeah. You here to help me stuff mailboxes?"

"I was thinking it might go better if we hit some minimalls. Put the flyers on people's windshields."

I studied his face. "I can't pay you."

"Did you hear me negotiating a price?"

"You're just here because you're a nice guy?"

His mouth curled into a half smile. "Don't push it."

As we drove to our first destination, I sketched him a quick background on the *lovely* turn of events with my mom, and he told me about the big argument his mother and Alison had had.

"Alison wanted to move the room-cleaning to

another day so she could come and help you." He blew out an exhale. "But when my mom gets something in her head . . ."

"Oh, it's nice she tried. But I kind of like this chauffeur service, too. Especially since it's finally for a reasonable rate," I said, and glanced out the window so I wouldn't catch a look from him that made me smile too big again.

A girl had to be careful. Especially when the guy who was making her feel weird was just a friend. And sometimes, not even that. Besides, I figured Jared had simply come by because Alison had asked him to. Her version of sloppy seconds.

I was impressed, but a little disappointed, too. It would have been nice to think that he cared enough to come over on his own.

Traffic slowed as we approached Thurman Oaks Park. People spilled out of parked cars, carrying kids on their shoulders, pushing strollers, holding hands.

Jared snuck me a look. "Hey, today's the farmers' market, isn't it? People come from all over . . . including some who might need a realtor." He glanced in the rearview mirror, threw the car into reverse, and backed up to the curb.

"Smooth," I said. I was still a little surprised I didn't have to shell out for this trip. "Thanks for being so nice—you know, helping me and all."

He did this exaggerated shudder. "Okay, enough with the nice-guy thing. Don't you know what people say about nice guys? Not only do they finish last, but they never get the girl."

I studied his face. Was there a girl in question? Or was that just a general statement? For lack of a better response, I let out a little "Sorry."

He flashed a grin. White, toothy. And, well, nice. Which set off something also very nice inside me. That I didn't want to think about.

I jumped out, took in the sweet breeze—peaches or nectarines from the booths, no doubt—and split the neon flyers into two piles. Handing one to him, I pointed toward a row of cars.

"You take that side, I'll take this one," I said, and to my surprise, he nodded and got to work.

We plastered the bright pink flyers on the windshields of every car in the lot, as well as dozens up and down the side street. Tossing the remaining flyers onto his passenger seat later, Jared nodded toward the midway and its colorful canopied booths.

"Five or ten minutes?" he asked. "Just to see if they've got snow cones or cotton candy?"

"More likely asparagus and blueberries, but why not?"

We pushed our way through the crowds, pausing to examine the fruits, veggies, nuts, and whole-grain breads. Venders' voices competed in promoting their specials and deals, most faces lined and bronzed from too much sun.

Jared settled on a package of pralines and was

turning to head out when something seemed to catch his eye. He stepped closer to me and gave my side a nudge.

I followed his line of vision. Massive and pulsating, a red, blue, and yellow inflatable obstacle course filled a back lot, wheezing and breathing from pumped-in air, as if it had a life of its own. Except it also seemed quite lonely with only one kid visible, straddling its climbing wall.

An attendant stood beside a $3.00 PER PERSON sign.

Jared flashed me that smile again. "What do you say?"

I shrugged.

"Come on, it'll be like we're little kids. At Gymboree or some rich kid's birthday party."

I bit my tongue to keep from blurting out, "Like yours?" He was being too nice to deserve any more of my mouth.

Instead I arched a brow. "You paying?"

"Sure. I'll do one better than that. I'll race you over the course. You win, I'll buy you lunch. I win . . ."

My interest and adrenaline skyrocketed.

". . . you have to wash my car." He studied my face. "In a bikini."

Yeah, right. Even so, I was surprised he'd think of me like that.

"Okay," I said, and high-fived him. I was pretty sure my volleyball skills wouldn't fail me, and there was no way I'd let myself lose and give Jared the chance to laugh at my scrawny bikini-clad body. "You're on!"

Jared forked over the bucks and we kicked off our

shoes and lined up on the platform. Two ropes stretched down from the eight-foot climbing wall, daring us to start.

"No rules," he announced. "Just stay on course, and first one to the other side wins."

We gave each other the Squinty Eye.

"Okay," I said. "Ready . . . set . . . *go!*"

I shimmied up the rope, my feet horizontally scaling the wall, and I reached the top. Piece of cake. I didn't bother to glance over, but my peripheral vision told me that he was somewhere behind, and my common sense added that he had a lot more weight to haul.

I used my back to slide down the steep incline, landed square on two feet, and turned to face a short tunnel.

Jared pounded the flooring beside me—throwing me up a good foot into the air—and then dropped to his knees and dove headfirst into his tunnel. Man, he was fast. . . .

After regaining my balance, I went on hands and knees through my (hot, stuffy) tunnel, coming out to see stacks of pumped-up horizontal pillars. Jared was in midair, doing a move worthy of a long jumper. I caught my breath and followed with a belly-up dive. Twisted in the air as I scaled the pillars, I thought I would somehow land on my feet.

Wrong.

I landed face-first. Wedged in a small space between the pillars and another climbing wall. On top of Jared.

Twin emotions vied for dominance. How totally

embarrassed I was. And how totally, weirdly good it felt to be so close to him.

He emitted a little groan, letting me know my full-body slam dunk hadn't killed him. But he didn't move. Didn't shove me aside and take advantage of my prone position for the easy win.

"Sorry," I said halfheartedly.

"You've got a lot of oomph for someone so little."

I nodded and sat up. Then, catching the mischievous look in his eye, I dove for the next wall, digging my hands into the climb moldings.

Movement blurred in my side vision, but I'd been an athlete long enough to know not to waste precious seconds sizing up the competition.

I dug, I hauled, I elevated.

Loving every moment of this one-on-one physical challenge with Jared.

Finally, I crowned the wall. First. I saw the long slide to the finish and pushed off on my butt, my hands waving triumphantly over my head, only to see him bullet, face-first, right past me.

We landed seconds apart, but there was no denying he beat me out.

Ugh. I *so* didn't want to wash his car! Still, I growled with good humor. "Rematch?"

His chest heaved. "Not on your life. I might not win again."

Standing, I offered him my hand. "So we should just call this even, huh, and forget about the bet?"

"In your dreams, Nic."

I pulled him to his feet, but then, instead of breaking away, I gave his arm a playful shove. And he gave
me that smile from the car.

Beating me again, darn him.

In UR Face

In a perfect world—or even a semisane world—I would think my racecourse challenge with Jared made me feel less tense. Cleared the air. But since when was my world perfect?

As we smacked flyers on windshields and did handouts, I pretty much kept my distance. I figured he'd forget all about our car-wash bet, and even though we were having a lot of fun today, back at school, we'd go separate ways. So I had to protect myself *some*how.

Eventually the stack of flyers dwindled, as did my motivation.

"Want to hit BK?" he asked, crossing the parking lot.

"There? Again?"

"I like Whoppers."

I grinned, suddenly remembering a saying from Mom's previous incarnation as a Martha Stewart housewife.

"What?" he said, and elbowed me playfully in the side. "What are you smiling about?"

"Oh, you know what they say. If you are what you eat, then fast-food lovers are cheap, fast, and easy."

He laughed and lunged for me, his arm coming from behind to lock around my neck in a playful half nelson.

It didn't hurt. Anything but.

"So," he said, "if I'm, what? Cheap and easy—"

"Don't forget fast," I interrupted, and giggled.

He pulled me to the hard wall of his chest. Until all of me pushed up against all of him.

Oh, God.

"And so what does that make you?" he breathed down into my ear.

I had no smart response. I was paralyzed.

"What, I've quieted the mighty Nic Antonovich?"

I came back to life and I wriggled from his hold, then attempted a casual stroll over to the passenger-side door.

Even though embarrassment was sometimes my middle name, I'd surprised myself by that whole body/brain stall-out the instant he had grabbed hold of me. Like I'd short-circuited. The last time I'd been that close to him was during the Canadian incident, and I'd certainly held my own that time. What was wrong with me now?

Because, a voice in my head suddenly responded, *this is different.*

Several deep breaths later, we were more or less back to normal. (Whatever normal was.) As we sat in the drive-thru line, we talked about colleges—the ones he was thinking of applying to, and the fact that I was hoping for a volleyball scholarship to be able to go at all.

He inched the car forward. "Do you have any games this week?"

"Yeah, Wednesday."

"What time?"

"Four."

"In the gym?"

"Uh-huh."

"Maybe I'll come and watch."

For some reason, I was Tense City again. Not that I was self-conscious or worried his presence would throw off my game. But it seemed . . . unnatural. I mean, a week ago he wouldn't have acknowledged me if we'd body-slammed while rounding a corner.

Did he feel *sorry* for me now or something—the girl whose mother was struggling to keep the house? Was he stepping up to "help" me like he had by pulling me away from that guy on the beach last summer?

"Alison comes to most home games," I said, as if that

smoothed everything over. Because really, I did *not* need a big brother. "My mom, too."

He looked at me like I'd spoken Chinese.

"So, I'm covered," I said. "I won't be the only player without a cheering section or anything."

"I don't know what's going on in that head of yours, Nic, but if I come to your game, it's because I want to." His gaze drilled into mine. "And just to be perfectly clear, I came to help today because spending time with you is better than studying for my physics test. Alison doesn't even know I'm with you."

I bit down on my lip, not knowing how to reply. It was great that he'd gone out of his way for me. But I hoped Alison didn't see this as sneaking around behind her back—or leaving her out. (Okay, now I *was* sounding mental. Was I ever satisfied?)

"Plus," he went on, advancing the car to the window, "I want to see your mom get back on track. Get more properties and more clients. So you can go back to thinking about normal things. Like homework and volleyball and the homecoming dance."

I felt my eyebrows jack up. The homecoming dance? That was sure random.

He braked and handed some bills to the plump, motherly-looking BK employee.

"Why would I be thinking about the homecoming dance?" I asked the back of his head.

"Well," he said, his face still turned away, "you've got that dress—"

"Do you want ketchup?" the server asked.

Jared nodded.

"Salt?" she asked.

Jared threw me a questioning look.

I shrugged. The food was unimportant to me. What I wanted to know was why he'd brought up the dance. It almost sounded like he was going to ask me to be his date or something. Which would be totally weird.

He handed me the bag, and I caught his eye. "So you were saying about my dress?"

He put the car in gear. "Just that you've got it, and the homecoming dance is coming up," he said, and drove. "I thought it would be good if your mother was in a better place so you could concentrate on getting a date or whatever."

I held my breath, hoping that Jared would fill the void with some sort of explanation. But it didn't work. He just pulled into a parking space and grabbed his Whopper from the bag.

"A date," I said, feeling oddly deflated. "With who?"

"I don't know." His voice was small. "That's your business."

That was it? Everything inside me tightened. I knew I had no right to feel disappointed or irritated, but since when did feelings make sense?

"I suppose it could help to rub Rascal's nose in it," I said, bringing up the one name I knew would get a rise from him. "I mean, showing him that my dress and I don't need his refund, anyway."

He frowned, and little lines furrowed in his brow. "How would he know you were wearing it? Did he see the dress?"

"He's heard about it."

"From who?"

"From me."

Jared's gaze whipped toward mine. "You two have talked about the dress?"

"Of course."

"Why?"

"I didn't want to let him completely off the hook." When he didn't respond, I poked him in the bicep. "Do you have a problem with that?"

He shook his head. "I'm surprised he didn't mention it."

I let his words sink in. Then I laughed. "To you?"

"Yeah, to me. And the other guys. At billiards."

"Billiards?"

"You know, shooting pool. We're in a league at a coffeehouse on Moorpark. Have been for over a year. And it seems like every tournament, it comes down to him against me. And believe me, the guy shoots his mouth off about everything."

Confusion and disappointment tumbled into my strange mix of feelings. "So that's where the rivalry came up? So this thing between you . . . it's about playing pool?"

"Yeah. But it doesn't matter how it started."

And here I'd been stupid enough to start to think

that maybe, just maybe, the tension between them had something to do with me.

"You know, Nic, I was surprised last June, when you were suddenly without a date. Since I'd driven you to all those stores and everything, and I didn't have anything lined up myself. I could have, you know, stepped up."

And been my pity date?

The mortification was once again descending. How fast could I get away from this car?

I clutched the door handle.

"Where are you going?"

I turned back to him, trying to compose myself, to somehow bring this back to business. "I'm going to walk home. And put the rest of the flyers in mailboxes along the way."

"What?" Honest-to-God confusion clung to his words. "Nic? Did I say something wrong?"

I cranked the door open. "See ya."

"What's wrong?"

Something snapped inside me. I knew I was over-reacting, but I couldn't stop myself. All the embarrassment I'd suffered with him piled up—the free car rides, the printing, the manual labor he'd "donated" today. It was all charity.

"Maybe I don't need your pity, Jared McCreary! Or your big brother act. Just do me a favor and stop helping me out."

He swore under his breath and grabbed my forearm. Not hard enough to hurt me, but certainly enough to indicate his confusion. "Don't go," he said, his voice cracking.

I shook free, jumped out (leaving my lunch, but oh well), and slammed the door. My face felt as hot as the blood rushing through my veins.

Pounding the pavement in the direction of my house, I paused whenever I could get my thoughts together enough to open a mailbox and jam a flyer in. But mostly my senses were filled with the roar of Jared's V-8 as he crept along behind me.

"Come on!" he yelled through his open passenger window. "Nic, this is stupid!"

My own house was suddenly within sight. I wanted to run inside, fall down on my bed, and beat my fists into my pillow. Jared and Rascal's rivalry was about pool. Jared felt sorry for me—I was poor and dateless and he thought he should have been my mercy date.

I picked up my pace. Until he let out a frustrated growl and his tires screeched on by me.

Good.

Good! Just what I'd wanted. Right?

Then how come I felt like I couldn't breathe or swallow?

I watched, in a sort of muddied stupor, as the Camaro's taillights raced down my street. Until they stopped and went bright red right in front of my house.

After an endless moment, the car lurched forward and pulled in against the curb, behind a dark green minivan.

Jared jumped out and headed for my lawn.

Obviously to wait for me.

I picked up speed and made it to our property. But what I saw did not immediately compute: not one, but two guys on my front walk. Snarling at each other. Feet spread, chests aligned, barely enough space between them for me to attempt some heroic stay of execution.

The Ghost of Prom Past

"I told you," Jared spat at Rascal, his mouth pulled tight against his teeth. "She's off-limits."

Rascal shuffled his body weight on my front walk and grunted out a laugh. "Yeah? She told Kylie you're not even her boyfriend."

What in the world was Rascal even doing here?

Rascal must have felt my presence, because without tearing his gaze from Jared's, he called out to me. "Hey, Nicolette! Your bodyguard here seems to have a problem with me being on your property!"

I dropped the flyers in a pile on the lawn and moved

in closer. "Jared was just leaving, actually," I informed them both.

Rascal forced a laugh, then body-slammed Jared, whose face went all blotchy with anger. He swung out, his fist connecting with Rascal's nose, making a sickening crunching sound.

Ack! My hands slapped to my own nose with a cringe.

I braced for an explosion of blood. But Rascal just cradled his nose with one hand, and advanced on Jared with the other. "I'll kill you, McCreary!"

"Guys!" I screamed, jumping up and down, like that was going to make a difference. "Guys! Stop it! Before some neighbor calls the police or something!"

Rascal threw a punch, but the pain probably threw off his aim, because Jared ducked away easily. Then Jared responded with a right hook. Which skimmed the top of Rascal's head, knocking him to the ground.

I dove to Rascal's side on the pavement, scraping my knee, and threw myself over his chest. Then I glared up at Jared, a dare probably shimmering in my eyes. I wanted this fight over before someone really got hurt. "Jared, enough!"

"Nic," he said, wiping sweat and dirt off his forehead, his voice softening. "Nic."

"Just . . . go!" I cried. Beneath me, Rascal was scrambling to get up.

Jared's jaw knotted as if he had something more to

say but was chewing the words to keep them inside. He shrugged and turned toward his car.

I squirmed around over Rascal. Whose face was mere inches from mine. Wow. "You okay?"

"I will be. After I kill him."

"Forget about that," I said, pulling back.

He sat up, touching the side of his nose. He winced. "You got any ice?"

"Sure." I found my way to my feet.

"And a nice soft couch or someplace to rest my head?"

My brain scrambled. Mom would ground me for life if I brought a guy in when she wasn't home. Especially when that guy was the culprit behind the refrigerator list. But she'd also taught me to be kind and compassionate . . . and he *was* hurt.

"Yeah, sure," I said, and fished inside my purse for my keys.

We staggered toward the door. I got it open and helped him through.

"You're probably wondering why I came by here today," he said, leaning on me as if his legs might be injured too.

I nodded. Understatement of the Year.

"I wanted to talk to you about helping Jared and me put things right before the homecoming game so I don't get suspended."

My face must have reflected my total shock, because a slow smile crept over his face.

"And if you believe that, Nicolette, I've got some farmland to sell you in downtown L.A."

Once inside, I left Rascal on the living room couch and headed for the kitchen to grab a bag of ice and a couple of sodas. Plus, I wanted to make sure he didn't get anywhere near the Top Ten list.

The phone rang as I walked past it. A crazy voice in my head suggested it was Kylie, checking up on her guy. (Ha!) Or Jared, *demanding* that I throw Rascal out. (Double ha!)

I answered and was fall-on-my-face shocked to hear the snotty voice of my father's wife. "Your father," she said, in clipped tones. "Is he with you?"

"No," I said, then summoned a Caffeine-worthy flip tone. "Why, is he missing?"

"Not missing. Just not home. I came home from work early and thought I'd surprise the two of them."

"He probably took her to the park. Did you try his cell?"

"Of course," she huffed. "He appears to have it off. So I figured maybe he was on some secret mission. Like down in Thurman Oaks, giving you more money."

I stiffened. Did she know how to hit where it hurt, or what?

Murderous thoughts zipped through my head. But only briefly, because at that moment my life was too interesting to waste any more brain cells on her.

"Once you find my father and Autumn, have him

call me so I know everything's all right," I said, and hung up before she had the chance to respond.

I made my way back to the living room, placed the sodas on the coffee table, and sat down next to Rascal. Leaving plenty of space between us, but close enough to pass him the ice bag for his nose.

"Will you hold it for me?" he asked, reaching for my hand.

I let out a laugh—sounding nervous, probably— and scooted closer. His hand guided mine with the ice bag to his nose.

"So," I said, feeling the need to put some emotional distance between us, "how does Kylie feel about you coming by here today?"

"I wouldn't know," he responded, nasal but clear-toned. "Wouldn't she have to be my girlfriend for her opinion to matter?"

Hope floated up from somewhere deep inside me. "You mean she's not?"

His gaze dropped.

Which was great, since I was suddenly smiling so big I almost ripped the corners of my mouth. "What— what happened?"

"Oh, Nicolette," he said, sort of pretending to sob. "I'm too choked up to talk about it."

I waited until he met my eye. A smile erupted on his face. Boyish. Playful.

I let mine free, too.

"Okay," he said, and laughed. "Here's the thing.

Cherry told Harrison about Kylie cornering you yesterday. About being some kind of peacemakers between McCreary and me. I got pretty mad, had it out with her, she slammed the phone down, and that's been about it."

"So, you broke up?"

"I guess. Besides, she's been getting pretty possessive lately, telling me what to do and stuff. And when I want something from her . . . ," he said, and his voice went all smooth and silky, "suddenly she doesn't consider us all that serious. Can't have it both ways, you know?"

Hmmm . . . no, I didn't know. But that wasn't *my* problem.

"So since I had nothing going on today, I thought I'd come by your house, see what you were up to. See if it's true that you and McCreary really are just *friends*. And if I could take you out for ice cream or something."

Take me *out*? Like on *a date*? Was that a choir of heavenly angels I heard singing?

But wait.

Circuit overload! I'd only had mere seconds to process that Rascal and Kylie had been unhappy, had probably broken up, and that he'd decided to move on.

To me.

This would require hours, maybe days, of discussion with Alison and staring into space. But I had to say something now, to appear as an active inhabitant of planet Earth. So I forced out: "I'm surprised you even knew where I lived."

"I dropped you off that day in the rain. And anyway, here we are, just you, me, and my misshapen nose," he said, and angled his head so his gaze was like a laser beam into mine.

I laughed. "How *is* your nose? Feeling any better?"

He lowered the ice bag and rested it on the coffee table. "A little better," he said. "The ice helped. But I'm thinking your lips would be even better."

Uh—my what? I was near utter speechlessness.

"Kiss it," he said. "Come on."

A laugh bubbled up inside me. Not that *anything* was funny.

"My nose," he said. "Or my mouth." He leaned in toward me, his lips targeting a bull's-eye for mine.

My mind spun wildly. There were a hundred reasons, a thousand reasons, to stop him. "Don't do it," I even heard myself say. "Don't kiss me."

"Okay," he said, but kept inching closer.

Liar that he was.

That he'd been.

That he'd always be.

I knew I should turn away, run, do something.

But was it so wrong to be selfish? Just this once? I'd waited and waited for this kiss, I'd paid my dues. I'd earned it.

Then, with nothing but breath between our mouths, Rascal suddenly paused. Hovered. Hesitated.

The quiet before the storm? Second thoughts?

As abruptly as he'd stopped, he plowed forward, his mouth capturing mine. Cool lips, pressing hard.

Surrounded by a clean, masculine scent. His body squishing me back against the arm of the couch, his heart picking up speed.

"Rascal," I murmured, to my own embarrassment.

I put a wide-fingered hand on his neck and pushed into him, the way the girls did on *The O.C.* and in all the really good movies. The last thing I wanted was for him to think I was inexperienced and immature.

Then a sharp tug on the clasp of my shorts told me he thought me anything *but*.

"Hey!" I shouted.

He stopped, then pulled back and wiped his mouth on the back of his hand. "What?"

I just shot him a look.

"Okay," he answered with a lazy smile. "Why don't you fill me in on the rules?"

"The rules?"

"Yeah, what I need to say or do."

I tensed, a little voice in the back of my head warning me I wasn't going to like where he was going. So I froze. Said absolutely nothing. Waited for him to continue.

"I'll do whatever it takes."

I narrowed my eyes. "Can you go back in time and take me to your junior prom?"

A smile touched his mouth. "If I could, Nicolette. It's not like I had a great time."

My breath went shallow. "You . . . you regret how it turned out?"

"You know, I do. I let you down and ended up bored half to death."

Wow. Just like in my fantasies, Rascal was actually admitting he'd made a mistake! But funny, while the moment was indeed sweet, I'd been expecting cotton-candy sweet, instead of what I got, sort of red Twizzlers sweet.

"You and I," I said, "would have had an incredible time." *Probably.* At least, I thought so.

"Especially afterward, right?" he asked, all low and familiar.

"Well—"

He silenced me with a finger to my lips.

I puckered my lips and kissed it. Simply because I could.

A grin touched his mouth; then his voice went all sexy. "We may not be able to go back in time," he said, "but there's no reason to waste any more. We can have the after-party right now."

"Now?"

"Sure. We're into each other. McCreary's history, Kylie's out of the picture. No one's home. What's stopping us from taking our relationship to the next level?"

I covered a laugh. "The fact that we hardly know each other?"

He let out a tired sigh, leaned back on the sofa, lacing his fingers behind his head, and looked me dead in the eye. "This is the best way I can think of to get to know each other better."

I twisted my ring.

I'm not real proud of this, but I'd be lying if I said I didn't consider his offer for a millisecond. I mean, Rascal-and-me. It was what I'd been wanting more than anything.

But then I got real. Any relationship that started in bed—or on the couch—would be pretty lame. Mom didn't even need to have a saying or a plaque for me to know the wisdom on that one.

And the bottom line? I had a sneaking suspicion Rascal didn't want *me* (my heart, my soul, my undying devotion) as much as the physical me. (Though that realization almost made me feel good, in a twisted way.)

Still, I had to know for sure.

"Rascal, what if I said I wouldn't be ready for anything like that for a while? That I just wanted to be your girlfriend and take things slowly?"

He shrugged. "If that's what you want. But I promise, if you give me a chance, it won't take you long to pick up speed."

"Why's that?" I asked, biting back a smile.

"Well, you're used to a guy like McCreary. Who probably has no moves. You just don't realize right now what you're missing."

Top Ten Uses for an Unworn Prom Dress

#6

Use the beautiful pink material as a shroud after you die from complete and utter humiliation.

"McCreary?" I squeaked, slowly standing up. "Does this have to do with Jared?"

He dismissed my words with a wave of his hand. "No, I'm just into you, okay? You're cute, even if you're more 'a' than 't.'"

I inhaled deeply, but the dizziness in my head had nothing to do with excess O_2. I couldn't believe he was so shallow that he'd take this so-called feud with Jared *this* far. "I think it's time for you to leave."

He frowned so deeply that a ridge rose between his eyebrows. "Come on, Nicolette. Don't be like that. We were just starting to have fun."

I crossed my arms over my chest. "Forget it, Rascal. Go!"

"Come on," he repeated.

"What makes you think I'm kidding?"

He stood and shuffled toward the door, saying something about being ready whenever I was.

Short of putting my hands in my ears and humming, I blocked him from my senses. "Just go."

And finally, he did.

I slammed the door behind him and fell against it. Then slumped down into a limp mess on the floor.

Who'da thunk it? I'd had an incredible few hours with Jared. Totally made out with Rascal.

And it had been the worst day of my life.

The phone rang a few minutes later. I would have let the answering machine handle it, but I saw Alison's caller ID. She was one of the few people in the universe I felt like talking to.

I picked up and, instead of saying hello, just moaned, "Kill me now."

"That bad?"

"Worse." I lay down on the couch.

"Your mother got fired?"

I bristled, in no mood for a guessing game. "Rascal was here." I recapped his anger about the mall thing, and how he and Kylie had pretty much broken up. "One thing led to another and we started kissing—"

"Seriously?"

I heard a click, which I assumed was an earring as she brought the receiver closer for this Breaking News Alert.

"And suddenly he was tackling me like we were on the five-yard line and I had the ball." I grunted. "Then he gives me this whole line about how this would be a good way to get to know each other better. Like I was a complete and total idiot."

"And . . ."

"And nothing. I threw him out."

A deep voice cut in. "Good."

The world tilted off its axis, leaving me dangling in confusion. Huh? Jared? When had he picked up the phone? How much had he heard?

"Jared!" Alison cried. "What are you doing? Hang up!"

"Not yet," he said. "I need to talk to Nic."

"Mom!" she whined loudly into the background. "Jared picked up the extension on my call!" After a pause, she screamed, "Mom!" again.

"I never should have left you two alone," he grumbled.

At almost the same moment, Alison told me to hold on, followed by the thump of her phone.

"So, Jared," I said, in this case figuring a strong offense was better than a defense, "not only are you a bully, but you're an eavesdropper, too!"

"Look, I'm sorry. But I had to hear what happened."

"Well, are you satisfied?"

"No. This only makes me want to go find him and beat the crap out of him again."

I couldn't help hoping this had to do with us, our moment on the obstacle course, our face-to-face in the BK parking lot. Even if I was pretty sure I was kidding myself.

"Look," he went on, "you know how Keith and Mitch and those guys were joking? How you were 'paying' me to drive you around places? Rascal is such an idiot . . . that's probably why he came by your house today."

I knew the friends with benefits thing could have been hazardous, but I still didn't take it very seriously. It was a joke! "And you know this . . . how?"

"Because I know how Rascal thinks, and he would take advantage of any situation. You've got to see that by now."

Alison broke in. "Are you done yet, Jared? Mom says you—"

"Look, Nic," he pressed on, ignoring his sister, "do yourself a favor and stay away from him, okay? He's trouble."

As if I didn't know that! As if I hadn't wanted to hate him since June 7 at approximately three o'clock. I'd been trying. But didn't Jared realize that sometimes the heart made decisions that the head didn't go with?

"Oh, okay, now that you've put it that way, I'll be sure to duck whenever I see him." I couldn't keep the snotty tone out of my voice.

He exhaled. "Whatever. I'm hanging up. See you around. Or not."

I couldn't help snickering at how dramatic he was being. Of course I would see him around. He was my best friend's brother.

I heard a click; then Alison apologized.

"It's okay," I said, surprised to realize it actually was. Deep down, I kinda liked it that he cared. Sort of like a brother. Still . . . it was different from on the beach last summer.

"But what I'm not getting here," Alison went on, "is what he meant about not leaving the two of you alone. Was Jared at your house today, too?"

After a moment of embarrassed silence, my voice quavered. "Well, yeah. He helped me hand out flyers since you were stuck cleaning your room. I—I thought you knew that," I said, telling a little white lie. I mean, I *had* thought she'd known. Until Jared told me differently.

"No," she said simply.

"I hope you don't mind," I managed.

A call-waiting beep bleeped over her response, but maybe that was for the best? Since nothing like that was ever going to happen again. I told her I'd better take the other call in case it was my mom, and we said bye. Cheerfully enough, I thought.

"Hello?" I said again immediately.

"Hey, Nicki, how's my girl?"

Great. Now I'd really won the lottery. "Hi, Dad." I knew I should be relieved that he was no longer "missing," but honestly, I hadn't been worried. If I lived 24/7 with Caffeine, I'd go AWOL now and then, too.

"Sorry about Cathleen's call earlier," he said, in a fast, dismissive way that told me not to probe. "I took Autumn to the beach, and we went out of cell phone range."

"Yeah, I figured it was something like that."

"So how did it go at the bank?"

I sat up. "Fine. They took the check, no problem."

"Did you tell your mother it's paid?"

"Yeah, last night."

"Did she believe the money was yours?"

"Yeah," I answered, then, wanting to steer the subject away before I had to admit that she'd showered me with appreciation and guilt, I asked how the kid was doing. Even used her name.

He hesitated.

The funny thing was, the longer he stayed quiet, the more my stomach tightened. "Is," I managed, "she okay? Not sick or anything?"

"No. No, she's fine."

I let out a breath I didn't realize I'd been holding.

"I was just surprised you'd ask about her. I hope it doesn't have anything to do with what you talked about the other day, thinking I loved her more than you."

I bit down on my lip. I didn't have anything to say to that.

"Nicolette," he continued when I didn't respond, "you're almost a grown woman now, so headstrong and independent. While you still need a father, it's in a different way than a two-year-old does."

Okay, obviously he'd been thinking this through, been rehearsing. No way he'd let me cut in or change the subject. All I could do was sit tight and hope this heart-to-heart ended soon.

"So if I seem to be giving her more attention, it's because she still needs constant supervision for her safety. Not because she's any more interesting or important than you."

I understood that my dad was trying to reach out, but it didn't make me feel any more included in his life.

The front door opened and Mom blew in, a stuffed briefcase clutched to her chest. I looked for a hint of a smile in her face, hoping the client had liked one of the properties. But all I saw was exhaustion.

"Oh, here's Mom," I said, knowing how to put an end to this conversation—fast. "Want to talk to her?"

Mom's eyes widened. Over the past few years, she and Dad had found an arrangement that suited them perfectly. They'd truly been able to start over. By going back to being total strangers.

"No, no, that's fine," Dad said, his voice taking on an urgent tone. "Give her my best. And next time, it's your turn to call, okay, Nicki?"

I grimaced. "Sure, Dad."

Mom put her briefcase down as I hung up. "There's a stack of papers on the lawn. Know anything about that?"

Yikes. Thank God there was no wind.

"Oh, yeah," I answered. "A homework thing. I'll go pick them up."

She slumped into a chair as I started toward the door. "By the way, before you woke up, you got a call from some guy."

The hair rose on the back of my neck. I was sure it had been Rascal scoping out my plans for the day. I just had to hope he'd had the sense *not* to speak his name to my mother. "Oh, yeah?" I said, trying to be cool. "Who?"

"Someone named Mitch."

I didn't know whether to be relieved or irritated. Why was he suddenly buddying up to me? Why not call one of the smart kids? "Oh," I said to Mom. "He's in my Spanish class."

"He wanted you to call him back."

Well, I wanted a lot of things, too. Mitch could take a number and wait.

Frenemies

My locker was the unlikely center of the universe that next morning. Jared walked by it—twice—without meeting my eye. Mitch stopped to tell me how bored he'd been all weekend, how he couldn't seem to get any "action" going. Whatever that was supposed to mean. And not a word about Spanish.

And then Kylie showed up. She couldn't even wait until geometry for our big chat.

"So," she said, and tugged on my sleeve, "did you talk to Jared?"

I didn't laugh. Well, not very hard. "About?"

Her eye roll was like, *duh*! "The pizza thing."

"Did *you* talk to Rascal?"

She glanced down. "Yeah, well, he's not much for working things out with Jared."

You think? And especially not now, since he's wearing the imprint of Jared's fist on his face.

But all I did was nod.

"I was hoping that it went better with Jared, and that we could put our heads together and make this work," she went on, good friend that she was.

But I was a gazillion years past her games. "You *really* want to go to the homecoming dance, huh?"

She stared at my face for a long moment, maybe trying to figure out if I'd asked a trick question. "Game. I said homecoming game."

"But the dance is after the game."

She gave me another *duh* look (just in case I was silly enough to believe we were really becoming friends).

"What's your dress like?"

She bit on the inside of her mouth. "Incredible."

Score one for Jared—he sure called this right.

"Okay, maybe you just bring Jared to our caf table today and we force them to talk."

I nodded, as if that was an option, as if she hadn't beaten this subject beyond death. Then I arched a brow and let her have it. "Look, I see two problems with that plan. One, I'm not Jared's girlfriend, and never was. And two, you're not Rascal's girlfriend anymore. Why would either of them listen to us?"

"Not Rascal's girlfriend? Who told you *that*?"

"Who do you think?"

She didn't even try. Probably too taxing on her limited gray matter. Without a breath, she replied: "Well, whoever told you that was lying." She examined a fingernail. "Everything's fine."

My tongue ran over the roof of my mouth. That figured.

Later, settling into our geometry class, I caught Kylie's gaze in passing. "How's Rascal's nose?" I asked.

"Sore. How do you know about it?"

"I was there." I pointed to the knee I'd scraped on the pavement, but when I looked up, she was already two seats behind and one row over, plopping her books on her desk.

"Nicolette, don't you have anything better to do with your Sundays than go to school to watch football scrimmages?"

"That's what he *said*? That it happened here?"

Mr. Hammond told the class to settle down—meaning Kylie and me, I imagined, as all eyes seemed to be on us.

"He's a pretty good liar," I said, and imitated her best eye roll.

Hammond glared my way. He had dark hair and a thick unibrow that made him look like Bert from *Sesame Street*. It made me, on my good days, feel sort of sorry for him. Like spending his life teaching geometry wasn't bad enough.

I opened my notebook and pulled out my homework, then found a fresh sheet and scribbled:

If you want the truth, ask Jared.

I folded it up into a nice little square, waited until Hammond turned to write some useless equation on the board, and flung it on Kylie's desk.

A minute or so later, something hit my shoulder. I waited until the coast was clear, reached down, and picked up her reply.

Yeah, right. What's it like on your planet?

My heart started beating like a moth trapped under a jar. I wrote furiously.

On my planet, your boyfriend is telling people he's over you.

I threw it at her, then waited for the scoff or grunt or the flying reply.

Nothing.

Finally, I turned around.

The great Kylie Schoenbacher was acting as if she was paying attention to the teacher, but her eyes were as pink as her candy-colored lip gloss.

I shifted back around. Trying to feel the triumph my head told me I'd earned.

●

At lunch, Alison and I scarfed down chili cheese fries in the caf as I told her about the stuff with Kylie.

"I'll bet she's grilling Rascal right now. Making his life frigging miserable."

"Way to go, Chunky," I said, and grinned.

"You heard him call her that, too?"

"Yeah. Can you imagine?"

She shook her head and then scanned the room. I figured she was trying to find Kylie, but faces were hard to single out in the crowd—even if Kylie's was particularly well painted.

I licked some chili off a finger. "So, you think she'll find out he was at my house yesterday?"

"Only if someone else tells her. Any witnesses?"

"Just your brother."

I thought she'd nod. I mean, she already *knew* Jared had been there. But when I looked over, her expression had hardened. Making me think she either didn't like that he and I had been together, or that I was starting to sound like Jared was a regular fixture in my life, like we were *going out* or something.

I grabbed my water bottle and got real busy drinking.

Then it struck me that Jared hadn't pointedly ignored me or called me that annoying nickname for days. (Which I still hated, though it was definitely better than "Chunky.") But now, since our blowup, we were back to square one. As if the past week had never happened.

But it had. And unfortunately, instead of mending

fences, the past week had actually brought tensions to a boiling point. Between nearly everyone: Jared and me. Jared and Rascal. Rascal and Kylie. And Kylie and me.

•

While I was spinning my locker combo later, Rascal and his big red nose appeared beside me. My first instinct was to disappear inside the gray metal hole. Not because I was afraid. I was just, well, *done* with him.

"Nicolette," he said, looking down at me over broken blood vessels and nasal swelling.

I held my gaze even and my grin in check. "Hey."

"Look, I don't know if you heard, but Kylie and I worked things out," he said, moving in closer.

"Yeah, she told me."

"And you told her . . ." His voice trailed off in question.

"Nothing that's going to get you in serious trouble."

"See, I *knew* there was a reason I liked you."

I stared at him blankly.

"So what went down between you and me yesterday," he went on, "or should I say what *didn't* go down . . ."

I shrugged. "Is our little secret."

He grabbed my arm and held it. "You're okay, you know that? Maybe sometime, someday, you and me—"

I thrust up my hand, my palm rigid. "Stop while you're ahead, Rascal."

He let out a laugh, then turned and walked away.

For the first time, I didn't stare after him. I knew I'd never again quiver in his presence, or get all hung up on what could have been. Because now it *had* been. Okay, not the prom. But some of the other stuff I'd dreamed about. And it had been okay, but not fall-on-my-face fantastic. In fact, most of it had left me with a sort of raunchy aftertaste.

So when his best buddy, Harrison, tried to get my attention by putting his hand on my arm as I passed in the hall later, my first reaction was to shake him off and keep walking. "Nicolette," he said, and flicked his head toward an open classroom door. His pale green eyes (with little hazel specks, which seemed weird when you stared into them, but could probably grow on you) peered into me. "Can I talk to you for a minute?"

I knew Harrison about as well as I knew Orlando Bloom. The only thing he could possibly want was my assurance that I'd keep quiet about kissing Rascal. He was looking out for his friend, and since I *did* understand loyalty and friendships, I moved alongside him to the doorway.

"Don't worry," I told him. "Rascal and I already talked. Everything's fine, everything's forgotten."

"Great."

A slow smile crept to his face. One that seemed, well, kind of personal for two people who didn't really know each other. So I gave him a quick nod and turned away. Only to feel his hand on my arm again.

I tugged away but this time could not shake him loose. "What?" I said.

"Just because it didn't work out for you and Rascal doesn't mean you and I can't be friends."

"Friends?"

"Yeah. And I don't have a girlfriend to complicate things."

Complicate . . . oh, this was more than I could take. Way more. I wriggled free and walked off. Harrison called something after me, but I didn't hear and I didn't care.

•

Zoe was doing warm-up stretches when I shuffled into the locker room later. I was beat from the long day, but even with all the stuff going on in my life, I couldn't think of a place where I'd rather be than practice. I needed some mind-numbing, physically exhausting, plain old *girl* time. I didn't even care if Coach Luther spent the two hours screeching at me.

"Did you see Rascal's nose?" Zoe asked as I was pulling my hair back into a ponytail.

I nodded and asked her what she'd heard.

"A weekend football scrimmage. He's lucky he didn't break his neck."

"Did you hear that from Kylie?"

"No. At my lunch table. Kylie hasn't spoken to me since I didn't show up for the group facial, remember?" Her dark eyebrows came together. "A hundred bucks just to wash your face. As if."

The furrow in her brow didn't soften as she resumed her stretches. In fact, when she glanced at me moments later, she looked downright bummed out.

"Something wrong, Zoe?" I felt I had to ask.

She shrugged. "Other than how my relationship with Matt seems to be disintegrating?"

I sat down on the bench. Not so close as to invade her body space, but close enough to let her know I cared if she wanted to talk.

"It's like he only wants me for one thing. Like today, he was going to pick me up after practice? We were going to go to his house for a while, you know?" she said, and almost smiled.

I did know, and realized Zoe's relationship was a gazillion miles more advanced than anything I'd ever experienced.

"Then he found out his mom was going to be home. Suddenly he's not picking me up . . . he's all like, what's the point?" She squinted so hard it looked painful. "He's making me feel like one of those friends with benefits couples." Then she interrupted herself. "Oh," she said, touching my arm. "Not that there's anything wrong with that, if that's what you're into."

I studied the guilt etched in her brow. Moments passed while my thoughts gelled.

She meant Jared and me. . . . Oh God, she *believed* those stupid rumors! Did that mean other people did, too?

Gossip Boys

Suddenly things made sense. Rascal on my doorstep. Mitch wanting to be "study buddies." Harrison wanting to be "friends." They were getting in line for their turn, to get some of the goods they thought I was giving Jared.

And the thing was, short of pleading my innocence, there was very little I could do. Sure, I'd straightened Zoe out, but that was like putting a Band-Aid over a gushing wound.

I threw my frustrations into my practice, slamming ball after ball. Coach Luther actually complimented me as she dismissed us, calling me a player who was "giving it her all." I just hoped the other girls weren't thinking I was giving my all to the male student body, too.

That night, I did my homework at the kitchen table while my mom worked on her laptop. Even though she kept biting her lower lip in frustration, I kind of liked just being near her.

By the time I closed my geometry book, it was too late to call Alison. Or maybe I'd delayed the call on purpose because, while I knew she would try to make me feel better about the friends with benefits thing, I didn't really want to talk about it, to give her *more* reason to suspect things were changing between Jared and me.

Lying in bed later, I tried telling myself that there were worse things that could be said about a person— although I had trouble thinking of many.

When the clock flashed midnight, however, I decided I had better do *something* or I'd never sleep. Talking to Jared was the obvious course of action. But it was way too late to call. Pulling him over for a sudden heart-to-heart at school would most definitely be a disaster. So I got up, turned on my desk lamp, and wrote him a note I could fold up and slide under his windshield wiper:

Call me. Stuff's going on. We need to talk. Nic.

The next morning, energy hummed in my chest as I rounded the block to the street Jared parked on. I might not have happened upon a miracle cure, but I was doing *something* toward the betterment of my reputation and to settle the unspoken static between Alison and me.

All this internal rambling was probably why the sharp pebbles of broken glass on the sidewalk up ahead didn't automatically register as disaster. I looked out at more glass on the street, and then the angry, splintered hole in Jared's windshield, before I truly understood what I was seeing.

That was when I broke into a run toward the car, as if it was a dying person or something.

Jared's beloved Camaro. The windows were smashed. Glass glittered on the dashboard, the seats, the pavement.

And only one suspect came to mind.

Rushing toward the school office, I thought about how Rascal had told me his football coach sometimes ran early-morning practices. If there'd been one this morning, Rascal would have an alibi. But come on, *who* would have done this but Rascal and his idiot friends?

I ran through scenarios of how to report the crime. What to say and what *not* to say. As much as I wanted to rat Rascal out, there was an unwritten code that students held against authority, and the last thing I wanted to add to my list of problems was revenge for turning in a football player.

When I got to the office, however, I could see that the dirty work had already been done. A lady in a tennis outfit was talking in hushed tones with Principal Carmody, the words "smashed" and "group of boys" escaping the huddle.

Before I could take a breath, Jared blew into the office. His gaze flew past me and straight to Mr. Carmody. "Yeah," he said, storming toward the group. "That license plate you announced over the PA is mine. What happened?"

I tucked myself in between the counter and a photocopy machine to get out of the line of fire.

Mr. Carmody (practically bald, no doubt from pulling his hair out over stunts just like this) told Jared that his windows had been broken. He explained that this woman had dropped her kid off and was on her way home when she saw three guys running away from the Camaro with baseball bats. While she couldn't ID them, they were Caucasian, medium to big, and wore below-the-knee shorts and T-shirts.

Sounded like half the guys in the school. If you didn't know what I knew. Or what Jared knew.

Jared stood ramrod straight, as if the overabundance of thoughts and emotions rushing through him needed every available inch. But when Mr. Carmody pressed him for possible suspects, he just shook his head. "No idea," he said, so convincingly that I almost believed him.

I swallowed my words. Part of me *wanted* Rascal called on the carpet. So this insanity would end. Rascal was the worst kind of bully: a bully with a lot of friends. What if they decided to go after Jared's head with the baseball bat next?

I couldn't stand it. I wiggled out of my corner, prepared to ruin my life to save Jared's—

But then he turned, caught my eye, and iced me with a glare. A glare with a distinct don't-you-dare flavor.

"Yes?" Mr. Carmody said to me. "Nicolette, isn't it?"

I nodded, my gaze still glued to Jared.

"Do you know who vandalized the car?" the principal asked.

My tongue was stuck to the roof of my mouth. I was confused, but I knew I couldn't snitch if Jared didn't want me to.

"No," I said, and reached into my pocket to weasel out the folded-up note. "Uh, here, Jared," I said, and passed it from my palm to his. "I just needed to give you this."

Mr. Carmody turned his back on me—obviously irritated about the interruption—and told Jared to accompany him outside to identify the car.

I stepped back to let them pass. Jared touched my arm as he moved by, in what felt like appreciation.

I watched his back as he left, hoping he knew what he was doing. Because I sure didn't.

It wasn't too hard to find out if there had been an early football practice. All I had to do was check out the nonsweaty, sleepy faces of the players just arriving.

Why was I not surprised?

Everybody (everybody!) talked about Jared and his car that day. Not just his friends, but people in my classes, in the halls, during morning break. At lunch.

Everybody, except Alison. Whose response at lunch was a shrug. "Yeah," she said. "I heard. Sucks to be him."

"You should have seen it," I pressed on, because obviously she didn't understand how serious it was. "Glass was *everywhere*."

"How convenient that you happened to pass by."

"Convenient?" I stopped chewing some cashews. "Are you implying I had something to do with it?"

"Not at all. It's just that everything Jared is involved in these days, you are, too."

"That's not fair." Adrenaline surged through my system, readying me for the defensive. Or offensive. Or whatever.

But she just shrugged and started talking about some new coffee place. And I acted like the subject change was normal.

Still, it would have been great to unload my feelings to my best friend that day. To own up to my worries and my knocking guilt about staying quiet.

And when a cinnamon-apple scent floated by my locker later, my first thought was that I was going to get that chance. With Kylie, of all people. I knew, more than anything else, that the homecoming-queen-to-be wanted peace between the guys—so *her* dress wouldn't hang beside mine in the Unworn Hall of Fame.

I turned to her, expecting an ally. Only to see a mascara-rimmed glare targeted straight at me.

"Stay away from Rascal."

Huh?

"I know he was at your house on Sunday. I know Jared was there, and hit him. I know everything. And all I can say is if you even *look* at Rascal again, you'll be sorry!"

Considering half the school thought I was "benefiting" Jared, I couldn't get too worked up over having Kylie or anyone else knowing I'd simply kissed Rascal during their breakup.

Although who told her was a curious mystery.

I decided to lob the ball back to her side of the court. "Come on, Kylie—what are you going to do, go to the prom with him again?"

But her scowl didn't break. Go figure.

"No—I'm going to have a nice long conversation with Coach Luther."

Huh? Okay, I'd lied to get out of a practice. But that *had* been for a good reason, and if need be, I could get Dad to vouch for me. And how would she even know? And then there was the friends with benefits rumor, but even if it *was* true, why would Luther care?

"What," I said, trying to sound all snotty right back, "are you even talking about?"

"Drinking on the beach. A certain digital photo?"

Whoa. How on earth did she get a copy of that?

"Oh, yeah?" I said, running a hand through my hair in what I hoped was a casual way. When all I could think was, no team, no starting position. No scholarship, no college.

"Yeah," she answered with a smug smile.

Crap. I couldn't risk her showing that photo to Luther. I had no choice but to work with her. "Look, Kylie," I said, and swallowed with my very dry mouth. "There's nothing between Rascal and me. I admit I had the mother of all crushes on him, but real life has a way of taking care of that sometimes."

Her face wrinkled like she smelled something foul. "You mean, you . . ."

Her voice trailed off, making me think that when she said she knew "everything," she meant the lawn but *not* the couch?

I decided to hold my cards closer to my chest. I had to give her enough to believe I was nonthreatening without admitting to anything . . . directly. "You don't have to worry about me. Okay?" I zeroed in on her squinty eyes. "And I don't have to worry about you showing that picture to Luther, right?"

She gave me something I took for a nod, then turned away.

I was dying to ask where the hell she'd gotten the picture, anyway, but I didn't want to rock the boat. Apparently she had good sources. And me in a tight spot.

•

I waited around at Alison's locker after the last bell, but when she didn't show, I had to hightail it to the locker room.

The team was doing warm-up laps when I shuffled

into the gym. Zoe slowed to let me fall into step with her, but I waved her on, saying I was tired.

Nothing personal, I just didn't feel like talking to anyone. Except maybe Alison. Could she possibly have stabbed me in the back? It was almost as if she'd set me up to take that photo, like someone had paid her to do it or something. Which was crazy. She had all the money she could ever want.

A few laps later, Zoe appeared beside me. "Okay, I'll tell you mine if you tell me yours."

"Huh?"

Sweat beaded her brow. "You seem upset. I'm upset. And don't they say misery loves company?"

A smile tugged at my mouth. Actually, it was nice that someone seemed to care. Still, I couldn't reveal the whole truth about my blue mood. I didn't even *know* the whole truth.

"It's Alison," I said, giving up what I felt I could. "She's, uh, been acting weird since I started spending time with her brother."

"That sucks," she said, huffing. "But you can't entirely blame her."

Yeah, except the beach picture happened way *before* Jared and I started hanging together. Back when I was swapping kisses with Canadian Guy and still moping over Rascal.

We rounded a corner of the gym and she added, "Still, it seems you two should be able to work it out. Get it out in the open, set some guidelines or something. Better than Matt and me, who are now done for good." She turned and looked at me. "He gave me the let's-be-friends line last night."

Ouch! "Oh, Zoe."

"I saw it coming, I really did." She inhaled through her nose. Bravely, I thought. "Still, to break up. And so close to the homecoming dance."

"Did you buy a dress already?"

"I was still saving."

"Well, that's good."

"I guess."

But getting dumped—dress or no dress—was definitely the pits.

Top Ten Uses for an Unworn Prom Dress

#5

Run the silky pink fabric up the school flagpole in solidarity with all girls who've been cruelly ditched, dodged, and dumped.

Zoe and I hung together for the rest of practice, doing drills, passing the ball, letting out long sighs. Later, we walked out together.

Leaning against an SUV in the teachers' parking lot was Jared. To say he was the last person I expected to see would be an exaggeration. That would have been my dad—or maybe Caffeine, if I could even remember what she looked like.

A smile tugging one side of his mouth, he crooked a finger at me.

"See you later," Zoe singsonged, and turned away.

I moved toward Jared, my pulse oddly elevated.

"Hey," I said.

"Hey yourself."

I understood the unspoken offer of a ride and figured it was better than walking. We silently climbed into his mom's car. After he started the engine, he turned to me.

"Your note. Sorry it took me so long to get back to you, with my windows and everything. What's up?"

I crossed one leg and then the other. I couldn't get comfortable. What had felt unbearable in the darkness had lessened during the course of this hectic and very confusing day. Still, I *had* to tell him. "Friends with benefits," I blurted out. "That's what people are calling us. I mean, not just as a joke. For real."

A full smile captured his face. But when he glanced back my way, his gaze was appropriately stony. "Yeah. I'll talk to Keith and Mitch and those guys."

He put the car in gear and backed out of the spot in silence, then pulled onto the main road.

"You know, Jared, Mitch has been calling me."

"What?"

"Yeah. Wanting to get together. Probably wanting . . . well, I don't have to spell it out, do I?"

A muscle in his jaw twitched. "I'll handle him."

"And Harrison."

He came to a full stop at a yield sign, and suddenly his eyes were all over my face. "Him, too? Crap, this has really gotten crazy. Don't worry. I'll take care of it."

"Not like you did with Rascal—okay?"

He exhaled, then nodded.

"You need to explain how a stupid joke got out of hand. And how you and I aren't even really friends anyway."

Jared leaned over and adjusted the AC. His hand came within inches of my knee, but just like the guy himself, it kept a straight course.

"Today, in the office. Thanks for keeping your mouth shut about Rascal."

I felt myself nodding, but the real Nicolette seemed to be lost somewhere inside my head, hiding among the twisted thoughts. I knew that somehow getting things right with Jared was of major importance, and yet I couldn't get past his mercy date offer. I didn't want to be Alison's-friend-that-he-should-be-nice-to. Or poor-Nic-with-the-virgin-prom-dress. I realized I wanted to be important to him because I was me. And I wasn't sure what to make of that.

He made a lane change. "And in the car the other day . . . you got mad and everything. I was stupid. Can we forget about that?"

"Yeah, sure," I said, then took a leap to safer ground. "As long as you can forget about this stupid feud with Rascal. I mean, you're not going to jump him or break *his* windows or anything—right?"

He flipped down his visor to block the late-afternoon sun. "Yeah, this thing's gotten crazy. If it goes any further, one of us will get expelled or arrested. I don't want it to be me.

"And the thing is," he went on, glancing my way, "I already played my next card. Kylie grabbed me and fired questions about Rascal and what really happened on Sunday. So I told her. It seemed like payback, even if it was pretty weak."

Of course—it was him. I'd told her to ask him what had happened. I laced my fingers in my lap. "Did you tell her what went on after Rascal came inside my house?"

"How could I? I don't know . . . I don't want to know."

"But you listened in on my conversation with Alison."

"Did I?" A frown and a smile had a collision on his face, the smile barely winning out. "Look, I'm not about making things harder for you. I just want you to be done with Rascal once and for all." He steered the SUV to the curb in front of my house and stopped, turning to look at me. "You *are* done with him, aren't you, Nic?"

"Totally."

"Okay, then."

He gazed my way, and I swear, I saw a sparkle. And it made something fizzy happen inside me.

"Okay." I knew I should grab the door handle. That we were *done*. Friends again. But I couldn't get myself to go.

I let the air between us hang heavy—silent—hoping my trick of saying nothing would prompt him to say something. Or *do* something . . .

His fingers made a drumming noise on the steering wheel. I got the message, loud and clear.

Hiding any signs of disappointment, I grabbed the door handle. "Thanks for the ride, Jared."

"That's what friends are for."

Mom stood up from a dining room chair when she saw me. A hand rigidly attached to her hip. I gave halfhearted thought to what incredibly delicious meal she was making for her one-in-a-million daughter tonight, and was vaguely disappointed when my deep inhale only came up with the piney aroma of furniture polish.

"What's for dinner?" I said, falling into a chair.

She jerked a neon sheet of paper in the air. The same color as the flyers Jared, Alison, and I had made.

I would have smiled had her mouth not been an angry red slash. "A prospective client brought this into the office today, Nicolette. Asking for 'Thurman Oaks' top-selling realtor.'"

Uh-oh. So that wasn't such a brilliant idea?

"Since that title happens to belong to a *man* from another firm on the other side of town, Nicolette, the receptionist called my boss over."

I swallowed hard, the enormity of my "good deed" settling over me.

"Who nearly popped blood vessels. Then called *me* over for an explanation. Which, of course, I couldn't give. Until I remembered the stack of hot pink papers on the grass last weekend. That you said had something to do with your homework?"

I cringed.

"Was it your assignment to commit false advertising? Or to see if you could get your mother *fired*?"

Shock waves formed before my eyes. "You—you got fired?"

"Not yet. But I'm on suspension, pending an investigation."

I pulled my knees up to my chin, wanting to hide inside myself. But even a thick turtle shell wouldn't have been good enough to hide me from my own stupidity. I'd wanted to help Mom so badly that I hadn't stopped to connect the dots . . . that, oh yeah, someone probably *was* the area's top realtor.

"It was supposed to be a surprise," I said miserably. "A good surprise. A helpful one. Like paying the mortgage, you know?"

(Okay, I admit the mention of the mortgage was to try to douse her flames.)

"That's what's so shocking about this," Mom said, her face all blotchy. "You were so thoughtful about the mortgage. And yet so thought*less* about this. Explain that to me, will you?"

Thanks, but I'd prefer Door #2, which I was sure was "crawl into a hole and die." I knew this was a line-in-the-sand moment, where I either barfed out the whole truth . . . or I could no longer live with myself.

"Mom," I began, looking at her through squinted eyes. "About the mortgage . . ."

Minutes later, I sat perched on the kitchen stool with the telephone pressed against my ear, listening to Mom go off on Dad. She was on the cordless in the living room, and Dad was in Ventura, although it seemed to me my mother's screeches could have been heard quite clearly without instrumentation in any part of Southern California.

"How *dare* you conspire behind my back!" she bellowed.

"Lynn," my dad said, trying to be heard from his end. "I didn't give her the money because I was teaming up against you. I gave it to her because she was right when she said I'd shirked my responsibility with the two of you. I should have paid you alimony longer, helped out until you were solidly on your feet."

"So now you're calling me a failure!" my mom wailed.

Oh, God. Just kill me now.

After a time, Mom told Dad she'd be paying him back. Every red cent. Then she hung up and stormed toward the back of the house.

I sat on the stool, my limbs quaking, just Dad and me on the line.

He spoke my name. My full name, I might add, although right then I would have answered to Nicki. Or Bonehead. Or any old thing he wanted.

"There's something I wanted to clear up with you," he continued. "I've been thinking that my decision to stay home with Autumn might be rubbing you the wrong way, since I missed so much of your childhood."

Whoa—a two-pronged acknowledgment: that I might feel sensitive, and that he'd missed my childhood. If my guilt hadn't been weighing me so low to the ground, I might have floated.

"What happened is that right before she was born, the company downsized. I got laid off. It made the decision a whole lot easier."

He paused and so did I. For a crazy moment, I thought I could hear his heart pounding.

"The money I gave you was Cathleen's. That's why I postdated the check. I had to make sure she was okay with it."

"Was she?" I asked, my voice sounding scratchy and like it belonged to someone else, someone who was kinder and more accepting of her parents' problems.

"Not really, but she allowed the check to clear."

"Well, you can tell her she's getting paid back." My words tumbled out. "Somehow." If not by Mom, then by me. I'd get a job if I had to.

"I should have told you this earlier. But the truth is, it turned out I liked being a stay-at-home dad, and practically had myself convinced that I'd chosen it."

I read something past tense into his tone. "Liked? As in, it's over?"

He made a *mmm* sound of agreement. "I also wanted you to know that I'm putting Autumn in day care and going back to work," he said in a weary tone.

"Things . . . aren't great between Cathleen and me. Another income, another *perspective* might help smooth things out."

I didn't know much about marriages—especially considering that the only one I'd ever seen up close and personal had sunk like the *Titanic*—but it seemed that he'd be *adding* stress rather than taking it away.

"I started sending out résumés," Dad said, filling the dead air. "I should be working again soon. So if you and your mom need anything, I can be there for you."

I managed to thank him, to get off the phone before saying anything *else* I'd live to regret. Then I shuffled out into the living room, knowing I needed to go see Mom (and grovel).

All this parent stuff (and the confusion and guilt) made me feel like a little kid again. Or at least made me wish I still was one. Made me wish for a quick fix like a hug from a grown-up, made me wish for a security blanket.

Top Ten Uses for an Unworn Prom Dress

#4

Cuddle material; insert thumb in mouth, and do your best Linus impression until you can feel and act your age again.

I got up fifteen minutes early the next morning and padded to the kitchen. Instead of grabbing my usual yogurt spoon, I pulled out a spatula and fry pan. Not for myself, but for my mom. I owed her big-time. *Waaay* more than bacon and scrambled eggs, but at the moment, a breakfast tray and an "I love you" were all I had to offer.

She smiled when I presented the tray to her in bed, and gave me a quick kiss. I suppose it made me feel a teeny bit better.

It wasn't long, though, before my emotions were

back on high. When I got to school and saw Alison at her locker, I marched up and asked, point-blank, about the digital photo of me on the beach.

"I told you," she said, turning toward me, defensive. "I deleted it."

"Well, apparently not soon enough. The Queen Bee has a copy."

"Not possible." Something obviously crossed her mind, because suddenly the lines in her forehead relaxed. "She's bluffing."

"How would she even *know* to bluff?" The bell rang, meaning we had five minutes to get to class. But I wanted to know *now*. I took a step closer. "What am I not getting here?"

"Look, Nic," she said, and bit on her lip. "It's true I took that picture on purpose. Thinking, well, I'd give you a hard time about showing it to Luther if you started acting all stupid over"—she threw a look around the crowded hallway—"you know who when we got back here."

I studied her scrunched-up face. "You would have done that?"

"Probably not. But at that moment, it seemed like something to try. A tough-love approach." She shrugged. "I mean, it's not like your mom's Top Ten list was working to remind you what a jerk he is."

I sighed, *not* a happy camper. But it did make sense. Alison hated Rascal for what he'd done to me. And she was there for me, in good times and bad. "Okay, so how did she get it?"

Alison shook her head. "You got me. I realized it was stupid and deleted it from the camera while we were still at the beach house."

She closed her locker. It drowned out the sound of my voice as I asked, "Then who did it?" But it didn't matter, anyway. There was only one other person who would have access to the camera. Who had been angry at me about Canadian Guy. Who clearly wanted to mess with me and my life.

And for the second time that week, I wanted to track Jared down—and wring his neck.

An hour later, out on a bathroom pass, I spotted Rascal on the Senior Bench.

I knew I'd promised Kylie I'd keep my distance. But I had a score to settle with him, too. And she'd never know, anyway.

I grabbed hold of his T-shirt sleeve and pulled him into an empty stairwell.

"Whoa," he said, shuffling beside me, letting his dimples run free. "You must want me *bad*."

I rolled my eyes and dropped my hand.

He pressed the back of his head and one foot against the wall. His nose was returning to normal color, and his smile was widening. "I knew you'd come around, Nicolette. I just didn't think it would be *at school*."

"Get over yourself. I want to talk about yesterday. About Jared's windows."

His foot came down hard on the linoleum. "That wasn't me."

"Oh, just stop." I glared at him, stunned that he'd think me *so* born yesterday.

But two could play at his game, so I took a Mother-May-I step to the other side of the Truth Planet. With silent thanks to the tennis mom who'd supplied the info, I described their appearances and outfits, and then laid it on the line. "You drop this thing with Jared, and I'll keep my mouth shut."

I was pretty sure I had his back against the wall. (More than literally.) Just as Kylie had my neck in a wringer.

Rascal gave me a cocky tilt of his head. "Say, just say, I admit it. And agree to back off. What happens if Jared comes after me? I can't fight back?"

"He won't."

"How do you know that?"

Because Jared was too smart to keep escalating this insanity. Because he'd let those things slip to Kylie, and he already thought he'd taken the last shot. But I wasn't letting on to *that*. "Because he told me," I simply said. "And he's a man of his word."

"And I'm not?"

The world before me went hazy. All I could think was, if my life was a sitcom, the studio audience would be howling with laughter. But I had to keep my focus. This conversation was about calling a cease-fire. Not about me or my dashed dreams (which didn't seem so dashed anymore, anyway).

"Rascal, just tell me you'll leave Jared alone."

His mouth puckered like he'd tasted something sour. But then he nodded.

I offered a hand. "Okay, then. And I'll promise not to go to the principal or the police. Shake on it?"

"I'd rather we kiss."

I rolled my eyes. The thought was not even tempting.

I half expected a James Bond–esque response like "Never say never again," but instead he took my hand and shook. "Fine," he said. "Besides, I need to try to smooth things over with Kylie, especially with home-coming coming up."

I assumed he didn't catch the irony in that statement. I just looked his way and said, "Yeah, I hear she's got a killer dress," and turned toward my classroom.

•

I went to Alison's locker after my last class, but again, she was a no-show.

Heading toward the gym, I spotted Jared in passing. I stopped him with a tug on his backpack, exhaled, and let rip. I told him exactly what I thought of him downloading the photo and sending it to friends back here in Thurman Oaks. (I was betting the Three Musketeers were involved.)

But he wouldn't give an inch. He stubbornly, thoroughly, and convincingly denied all knowledge or participation. Then walked off, leaving me with my fingernail in my mouth and my tail between my legs.

I didn't know *what* to think.

Zoe welcomed me with a big smile when I traipsed into the locker room later. Her full focus felt terrific, momentarily filling the little hole in my best-friend heart.

"Ask me what's new," she bubbled.

"Okay. What's new?"

"Ben Snyder asked me to the homecoming dance!"

I wasn't quite sure who he was or if she even liked him. But I held up my hand for a high five.

Luther's voice suddenly filled the air, painstakingly reminding us that we'd lost our last two games and that she was not coaching a team of losers. So we'd better win today's!

Her warning still rang in my head as I crossed into the gym. The house lights were on, the nets erected, and a sprinkling of onlookers gathered on the court and bleachers.

The starters fell into position and passed the ball around. I couldn't help thinking that the ball was a sort of symbol for how I'd been feeling lately. Slamming back and forth between Jared and Rascal, between Mom and Dad, with occasional setups from Alison and Kylie . . .

Some time later, I spotted my mother climbing the bleachers. While her loud cheering sometimes embarrassed me, it warmed my heart to see her today. She still loved me, even though I'd been screwing up her life. I waited until she caught my eye, waved, and mouthed "Hello." I only hoped Alison would roll in, too.

The referee blew the first whistle, and we did a pregame handshake with the other starters, followed by our respective cheers. The next whistle sounded and the ball went into play.

As setter, I could set any hitter with the ball, and unlike some other setters I'd watched, I did not play favorites. To me, a good game was all about stamina and teamwork. Whoever was on top of her game got the most sets. Trouble was, that day, *no one* was playing well.

But the worst of all?

Oh, that would be *me*. My setting was off, over the net, into the block.

In the third game, the ball was coming down right at me, so my arms automatically went over my head. The ball fell into my hands. Piece of cake. Like it had a gazillion times in practices and games. I went to launch it back up to my team. But the stiff fingers I relied on betrayed me. The ball continued falling. Right through my hands. Until it landed (ka-thunk!) on the hardwood.

The ref blew his whistle and signaled a point for the other team.

Ugh! Missing the ball was bad enough. But dropping? What was I, five years old?

A couple of girls on the other team smirked; one

was biting back a laugh. Complete humiliation. *Waaay* worse than losing the point. Or the browbeating I'd get from the coach later.

Zoe gave me this *I'm sorry* look. And a couple of minutes later, probably still trying to cheer me up, she pointed up to a bleacher area. "You've got a fan."

I looked up, dizzied, distracted, and set my eyes on a big, waving piece of cardboard with black-painted strokes:

GO NICOLETTE!

Beneath the cardboard extended a pair of jeaned legs. Alison had been wearing jeans earlier. My blood warmed. Everything was just fine. Once again, I was making too much out of things.

But the cardboard eased lower, and the face that appeared above it wasn't hers. Or even a girl's. It belonged to a too-handsome, dark-haired guy. With eyes the color of root beer and a crooked smile that I knew could light up his eyes. Who did things to my insides I was only now just beginning to understand.

Omigod, Jared.

"Antonovich!" barked an irate coachlike voice from the sideline.

I knew not to follow the voice, but to swivel my head back toward the net—and just in time, too, to take a serve with the center of my face.

My hands rushing up to cup my nose, I couldn't decide which would be worse: having it spurt like a red geyser in front of all these people who already thought I was a dork. Or simply having it swell purple until I looked like Rascal's ugly twin.

Don't Even Go There

After I'd sat out the last game of the set under an ice bag, it looked like my nose would retain its color. And its blood.

I got home to be greeted by Mom on the phone, retelling my volleyball/nose story. Not in a concerned motherly way, but light and friendly. I knew she had to be talking to Alison, so when she met my eye, I pointed at the phone. She nodded and said into the receiver, "Here, talk to her yourself," and handed it over.

"Hey," I said, then winced at the pain that came from an automatic smile.

"Glad you're okay," came the deep reply, the voice of my childhood.

Dad? Wait—Mom was talking to Dad? In a nonlethal, I-don't-want-to-rip-you-a-new-one way?

This was ginormously weird!

"Yeah," I managed to say into the receiver.

He asked a few questions about the game, but once I'd given him satisfactory answers, I turned the tables on him. Inquiring minds wanted to know! "Did you just happen to call tonight?"

"No, your mom called me."

"Why?"

"We had some business to discuss."

"Business? But last night you two . . ." My voice trailed off as I tried to find the politically correct term to recap Mom's rage and his attempts to calm her down.

"Yeah, well, she and I talked a few times today about refinancing the mortgage. Seems to make the most sense right now."

Relief overshadowed my shock. "Great," I said—and meant it. While I'd been totally ready to step up with the mortgage thing, I was more than happy to "be the kid again" and hand this responsibility to Dad. Besides, he'd be likely to make things better, unlike *moi*.

I got off the phone and helped Mom stir-fry some veggies. I kept thinking Alison would call . . . surely Jared had told her about my nose disaster? But after dinner, I couldn't wait any longer, so I decided to pick up the phone myself.

Jared answered.

Crazy as it seemed, my heart went all erratic.

"Hey, it's Nic," I managed.

"How's your nose?"

"Not as bad as Rascal's."

He laughed.

My accusations about the digital photo seemed to fly out the window. It was like they'd never happened. And it was no longer like talking to my best friend's older brother. Or a friend, even. Somehow, while I hadn't been looking, he'd stepped up to the role he'd once teased me about. He'd *become* an Extra-Hot Senior. And I was a lowly junior, trying to catch my shallow breath.

"Thanks for the sign today," I told him after a silence. "It was great."

"You're welcome. I'd originally planned to do something with bright colors at the print shop, but then suddenly I didn't have a car."

"I loved it just the way it was," I gushed.

Then I realized I'd said "loved." Not "liked" or "really liked." Did he notice, too?

"So," I said, and swallowed hard. "I was wondering if Alison was home?"

"She's in the shower. But I'll tell her you called."

"Okay, thanks." I bit my lip, giving him ample opportunity to take charge of the conversation—tell me stuff, ask me stuff (like *out*).

But again, no dice. He just said he'd see me tomorrow, and we disconnected.

"Yeah," I said. Then held the receiver against my cheek and let out a sigh.

•

Alison didn't call back. All night.

I tried not to keep looking at the clock. (How long could a shower *take*?) I tried not to overanalyze every aspect of our friendship—what I might have done to make her mad. I tried not to worry and/or care. But I failed on every point.

Taking gel and a brush to my hair the next morning, I ran through can-we-talk scenarios with Alison in my head. But since I didn't know what she would come back at me with, it was pretty hard to bring them to hug-and-make-up endings.

Alison didn't stop by my locker before first period. When I spotted her by a junk machine later, she suddenly got *very* busy studying her choices. I imagined her thinking: *Hmmm . . . M&M's or Skittles? Say hi to Nic or pretend not to see her?*

My head told me to catch a clue and walk on by. But my gut wouldn't give up that easily. This was *Alison*—who knew me better than anyone in the world, who knew that in my weakest moments I zipped inside The Dress and sang old Beatles songs. Alison, who'd seen me through so many tough days before.

"You'll be proud of me," I said, trying to break the ice.

After a silence so long I wondered if I'd celebrated a birthday, she looked up. Her expression flat, nonreadable. "Oh, and why is that?"

No! No, no, no. *no*. She was supposed to guess. But like a meteor had fallen from the sky and thunked my head, I realized that of course, she hadn't forgotten. She just wasn't playing.

I worked fast for something neutral so I could go off and regroup before I did something goofy like tear up. "I tackled my hair today instead of just throwing it back."

"Your hair? I thought you said you were over Rascal."

"I *am*."

"Oh, you're telling me your sudden interest in your hair isn't totally guy-related?"

I had thick skin for slams from girls like Kylie. But not from Alison. "Okay, fine, I was up early, worried about seeing you today. It's like you're avoiding me. You didn't come to my game yesterday. You didn't call me, even after I left a message. I did my hair this morning just to keep my hands busy while I thought about what to say to you."

There: the truth.

She grabbed a Snickers bar from the well of the machine and tore open the wrapper. "You're right," she said, and shrugged. "Jared did tell me, but I didn't call you back."

My heart jumped to my throat. No "I'm sorry"? Who *was* this redheaded girl? "We need to talk."

"About what? You and my brother?"

"Actually, about what's happening between you and me. I mean, Jared and I—"

"Spare me."

"Alison! It's not what you think."

"How would you know what I think? When practically the only McCreary you talk to these days is Jared?"

Hey—that wasn't fair. "It's not my fault you hide from me and don't call me back."

"Look," she said, "I'd love to stay and chat, but really, I think we're done here."

My mouth dropped open.

She turned and walked away. So very civilized. So in control.

Leaving me so incredibly heartbroken that I couldn't even stand to think about it. More heartbroken than any guy could possibly make me feel.

Top Ten Uses for an Unworn Prom Dress

#3

**Hang much-loved dress above Alison's
locker with the words "Best Friends Forever"
spray-painted on the fabric.**

That evening, Alison didn't call—again. Not that I really expected her to any more than I expected to wake up the next morning two inches taller or with a perfectly coiffed 'do. (But hey, a girl could dream.)

In fact, not only did I wake up still short and best-friend-challenged, but as I shuffled into the kitchen, I patted down what felt like Shredded Mini-Wheats on my head.

When my mother announced that my dad and Autumn were coming by later, I thought maybe my brain was malfunctioning, too.

"He's going to sign those re-fi papers," she added.

I swirled orange juice in my mouth to keep from blurting out the words charging through my head. *You're letting Dad and his spawn of the she-devil into our house?*

She popped rye bread into the toaster. "He apparently has a job interview down here as well."

I swallowed—hard. In the L.A. area? That would be one monster commute. Unless he sold the beige monstrosity and moved back this way. Or left Caffeine. Hmmm . . .

Then another thought hit, hammer hard. Where would Autumn be during this interview? "You're—we're—not baby-sitting the little brat, are we?"

Mom turned, little lines creasing her forehead. "No," she said, then seemed to consider it. "No, I'm sure he'll work that out. Although why *that woman* doesn't take more responsibility for her own child, I'll never know."

I got real busy tearing the seal off a carton of yogurt. No way was I risking putting my foot in my mouth again.

Besides, I knew what she meant about needing to take more responsibility. I was guilty there, too. Not with Dad or Autumn, but with Coach Luther. For as much as I wanted to believe Kylie would keep her promise and keep her big mouth shut, she was not one to be trusted. And the fact that I had *no idea* how she'd gotten a copy of that picture kept gnawing at my nerves.

A heart-to-heart with Luther had as much appeal as wisdom-tooth removal, but if I was lucky it might save me a lot of unnecessary pain, too. Though it was equally likely to backfire.

Alison and I pretended not to see each other in the halls at school. Which, if I allowed myself to think about it, did terrible things to my insides. But also made it less complicated to head toward Luther's office at the lunch bell.

"Antonovich," she uttered, crisp and controlled, looking up. "What can I do for you?"

My heart felt like it was thrashing around my rib cage, and I suddenly wanted to be anywhere but there. "Can I talk to you?"

At her direction, I sank down in the chair opposite her desk. Posters and calendars showing sports figures lined her walls, alongside photos of her with former Hillside players, and one of Luther herself in a college-volleyball uniform.

As if she had a life. Besides tormenting us.

I took a deep breath. "There's a picture of me going around. Holding a can of beer. I know something like that would be automatic grounds for expulsion off the team," I went on, my words coming out faster and faster, "but you need to know—you need to believe—that I was only holding it for someone else, that I don't drink and never have. And that being your starting center is, like, the most important thing in my whole life, the only thing that's going right."

I paused to breathe. And to squeeze the arms of the chair for protection from a sudden windstorm or spontaneous combustion or something.

"I assume," she merely said, "there's more to this story?"

"That's it," I managed.

"It? Come on, Antonovich. You can do better than that."

And so, simply, I did. I told her about the mortgage. My estranged father. Autumn. Caffeine. Hiring Jared to drive me. (Twice.) Which, of course, led to the tales about Rascal. The Dress. The prom I didn't attend. Kylie. The friends with benefits rumors. And Alison. Especially Alison. And how much it hurt to be at odds with my best friend.

By that point, tears filmed my eyes. When I was finally done, I let out a little hiccup-cough. And what remained of my pride. "More than you wanted to know, huh, Coach?"

Leaning back in her swivel chair, she steepled her fingers. A tense silence enveloped the room, making my lungs feel like they might burst. (And in the recesses of my mind, I could hear the crumbling of the volleyball scholarship letter that I'd once believed would be my yellow brick road.)

"If a picture of you with alcohol comes across this desk," she said, and pressed her lips together, "I'll be put between a rock and a hard place."

I shuddered, feeling terrible about distressing the woman I (secretly) lived to please.

"For the team's sake, and for your own."

Team . . . team . . . like I would still be on it?

"So let's take care of this right here and now. The official word is you've already explained the situation to me, how the picture was doctored to make it simply *look* like you were holding a beer. Am I clear? And in return for this favor, I will expect you . . ."

Her voice trailed off and her brow furrowed. But for once, she did not scare me. I'd do anything—even play smash ball with my sore nose—if it meant keeping my position.

Finally, she frowned. "You will skip practice today and go straight home. Turn off the phone, kick off your shoes, pop in your favorite DVD. And stop thinking about other people. Stop thinking, period. Just veg. All afternoon. All night. All weekend, if that's what it takes. So when you come to practice on Monday, your head is completely clear of family, friends, and problems. And back in this game."

"That's . . . it?"

"Nicolette," she said, her voice oddly gentle. (Nicolette. Not Antonovich?) "It sounds like you're going through enough."

My gaze traveled across her, wondering if another being had crossed the space-time continuum and entered her body. That was the only reasonable explanation.

"Now get out of here!" she suddenly bellowed. "Before I change my mind!"

A smile quivered at my mouth, and I ran like hell.

Going Nowhere Fast

Coach Luther's unexpected compassion so completely lifted my spirits that I couldn't even bum out too badly over Alison. But as I was stepping down the front steps after the last bell, my quasi–best friend appeared beside me and did a double take at my backpack. "Don't you have practice?"

My heart sped up. I *so* wanted to fall into a natural and normal conversation, *so* wanted our life back. "Luther gave me a Get Out of Practice Free card."

"Why?"

"I talked to her about the digital picture. Explained

it wasn't what it looked like. In case Kylie decided to go through with her blackmail threat."

Then I waited for Alison to grin. To nod. To do *something* besides continue glaring at me.

Finally, she said, "In other words, you're messing with Rascal again and covering your butt?"

Oh, come on—enough with this Rascal stuff! Did she really care? Or was it just easier to harp on any feelings I'd had for Rascal than for her brother?

"No," I said forcefully, and sighed. I mean, if anyone was guilty of anything here it was Alison, for taking the picture in the first place.

A noise burst from her mouth, half growl, half laugh, half groan. (You get the idea.) "When are you going to get that he totally used you? That he only asked you to the prom because he knew it would get back to Kylie, that she'd go berserk and come home?"

Numbly, I gave my ring a manic twist. Say . . . what?

"Yeah," she went on. "Kylie could have handled him going with *anyone* but you."

Her face swam before my eyes as I tried to take it in. Never—*never*—did I think Rascal had asked me for my beauty or status. I'd figured I was just the best of the slim pickings. But I couldn't ignore what she was saying. It *did* explain how I so suddenly became a bleep on his radar screen.

But Kylie hating me? Okay, maybe *a little* just

because the food-poisoning rumors she'd launched against me hadn't taken. But enough so she'd move back from Arizona? I couldn't believe I had that kind of power.

"Kylie didn't even *look* at me from, like, when we worked in the caf together until last week," I protested.

She held up her palms as if to say *duh!*

"What—the throwing-up thing?"

She nodded.

"That's crazy. She had the flu."

"Tell her that. And Rascal feeds off it, teases her. Think about her nickname, Nic. Chunky? Blowing *chunks*." She exhaled through her nose. "You were the only girl at Hillside she wouldn't tolerate taking her place."

A lump lodged in my throat, the size of, well, Arizona. "And you know this—how?"

"From Jared. Rascal shoots his mouth off when he plays pool."

Yeah, Jared told me.

Okay—assuming I believed this—that was *cold*. Ice cold. What would Rascal have done if his stunt had backfired and Kylie hadn't come home? Would he have stood me up?

A jab of pain from my ring finger told me to stop twisting and refocus. Besides, Rascal was a jerk. Kylie was an idiot. Why should this surprise me?

But it didn't take long to make the next logical connection. That Alison had not said a word to me. Until now. When she was mad.

"When?" I asked. "When did Jared hear this?"

"At the beginning of the summer."

"And he told you right away?"

She nodded.

"And you kept it from me?"

She shrugged, and for a moment the animosity died out of her tone. She sounded like my friend again. "You were already heartbroken. Why make it worse?"

I turned away to privately digest all this. I understood protecting a best friend. But I hated to think she had been keeping secrets while I had whined to her about my unrequited love and my unworn prom dress, probably looking like the superloser I was.

And Jared? He knew I'd been duped, too. And besides being furious at Rascal, did he feel sorry for me?

Oh, God . . .

Heat flared up my neck.

But in the midst of my humiliation, there was something left that wasn't adding up: Rascal and his roaming hands. "So if Rascal isn't into me at all, why'd he come over last Sunday?"

She pressed her lips together, as if choosing her words. "Jared says Rascal's been telling the guys that he's not getting enough from Kylie. So figure it out. There were rumors about you giving it up easy to my brother. Rascal already knew you kinda liked him. Either he was trying to get some on the side, or make Kylie jealous so she'd give in herself."

My thoughts cartwheeled. Knowing Rascal and his Teflon conscience, it was probably both. But as disheartening as this was, I couldn't think about it now.

I had to stay on Alison and me. While part of me (calmly, rationally) appreciated and understood why she'd kept this painful stuff from me, another part *really* resented it. And hated the fact that it had come out in anger.

"Thanks for finally telling me . . . I guess." I swallowed hard. "And I suppose we're even now."

"Even?"

"Yeah, since I've been making you crazy lately." I didn't say with her brother. I didn't have to. Let her do her head-in-the-sand act and think I meant Rascal if she wanted.

Besides, while it was true that Jared and I were spending time together, he was still only a friend. Whether I liked it or not. So why go rubbing salt in Alison's wounds when nothing was bound to change?

She grumbled something meaningless and walked away.

Maybe she needed a feet-up, clear-your-head weekend, too.

Mom wasn't home. But since she hadn't expected me to be home at this hour, either, she hadn't left a note.

I couldn't quite bring myself to unplug the phone, but I made myself a promise to only answer if Mom's cell number flashed on the caller ID. Or Dad's.

I grabbed a DVD off our shelf. *Bring It On*, where one best friend gets together with the other's brother, was usually a favorite, but now? It hit a little too close to home. Instead I popped in *Pirates of the Caribbean*.

Mom shuffled in the door sometime after five. The business suit and the heavy lines around her eyes announced that her outing had not been a pleasure cruise. I looked back at the TV. Part of me did *not* want to know.

"The bosses called me in," she said, and let out this scratchy sigh. "I've been put on a sixty-day suspension. At which time they will reevaluate my 'place in the company.' "

I paused the movie. Johnny Depp stood frozen with a devilish half grin. But believe me, no one *outside* the screen was smiling.

"You told them it was me, right? That you had nothing to do with the flyers?"

She nodded and leaned over to pat my arm. "Maybe it's for the best. Maybe I should take this as a sign to find a new job."

Considering how much she hated it and how bad she was at it? Uh, yeah! But what I said was "At least you have the time to look around some."

She moved toward the kitchen. Probably to make

something complicated and yummy that I totally did not deserve. I couldn't get my head back into the movie, so I followed to help.

As I pulled the silverware drawer open, my gaze drifted to the cluttered refrigerator door and a gaping hole in the midst of the photos/notes/coupons mess.

"The list," I said, and pointed to the mess. "It's gone."

"Oh, that—I was cleaning up last night and pitched it." She threw me an over-her-shoulder look. "It was just a joke, right?"

"Right." A joke. No matter how many so-called *uses* I'd come up with lately, I certainly hadn't committed them to paper. Still . . .

"I started thinking, honey," she said as she started pulling things out of the fridge, "that maybe it was wrong of me to get on you about that dress. Your first formal dress is very special, like a rite of passage. And since you didn't actually get to wear it, you should be able to keep it on the back of your door or wherever you like for as long as you like."

Emotion sort of jammed in my throat. Wow.

"You remember when Grandma died?" she continued, her question, of course, rhetorical. "Up in her attic, I found the dress I'd worn to my senior prom."

Her voice seemed to catch, but I would have set myself on fire before speaking what she was surely thinking, which was that her senior prom had been her first date with my dad.

"Grandma had kept it for me," Mom continued, "because that night had been so special."

I worked to find my voice, grappling with the unspoken tension and what she was trying to tell me. "So what you're saying is my hang-up about my prom dress . . . it's *hereditary*?"

Things That Go Bump in the Night

Frozen at the sink, Mom seemed to smile to herself. "I wouldn't go so far as to say hereditary. Safer to say lots of people attach emotions and memories to their possessions. But it is fitting that you bought your dress with money from Grandma, don't you think? She would have loved that dress as much as she loved mine."

I nodded, giving that warm thought a moment to penetrate. Then, getting back to Mom's dress, I asked what had happened to it.

"Unfortunately, the dress was ruined from the years

of heat up in the attic. The color had streaked and faded, the crinkly stuff underneath—"

"The crinoline," I volunteered.

"Crinoline. It had cracked. The whole thing was a mess."

A sudden flash of grief blew across her face. Making me think that she, too, was drawing the connection between the fate of her dress and the fate of her marriage.

Ugh.

Had I been a friend, I probably would have given her a hug. But I was the *product* of her regrettable marriage, for better or for worse. And this was *waaay* too much *yuck* for me to handle head-on.

"So you threw your dress out?" I asked, attempting to keep my head erect and the conversation light.

She nodded. "Nothing else I could do. But somewhere, I'm sure, there's a picture of me in it. I'll dig it up for you one of these days."

My words spilled out before I could catch them. "Only if you want to. I mean, if you think it wouldn't upset you."

Her lips curved, but there was no joy inside her smile. "It'll be good for me. That was then, and this is now. It's time I truly moved on."

Yeah. It probably was. But she wasn't going to hear that from me.

After a long moment, Mom gave her head a little shake. "But don't worry about yours. You've got that industrial-strength dress bag to protect it from the elements. Plus, we'll keep it out of the attic. Yours will live on forever."

I nodded. But saving The Dress forever didn't seem so important as simply having it right now. . . .

"But if you think you've got an obsession with your prom dress, Nicolette, just wait until you've got a wedding dress in your closet!"

We laughed and got busy making dinner—together.

Later, my belly filled, my good spirits gave way to worries again. I wondered where Alison had been all afternoon. Had she been out cultivating a new best friend?

I tried to sleep, but the darkness only made my thoughts bolder and, well, darker. I needed to talk to somebody, and for the first time since I was twelve, my best friend was out of the question.

Eventually, I bolted up, remembering I had Jared's cell phone number. A way to contact him exclusively— without getting Alison or waking up the whole house.

I raced through the darkness, careful to avoid the furniture, grabbed the phone, and punched in his number.

" 'Sup?" Jared's recorded voice answered. "Leave me a message." *Beep!*

So I did. "Hey, Jared, it's Nic," I said, trying to sound normal, like I called his cell at eleven o'clock every night. "Nothing important, just, uh, checking in." I ended idiotically that I'd see him on Monday at school.

And crawled back to bed. And worried that he hadn't picked up because he'd seen it was me who was calling.

I tried to smother my mile-a-minute brain with my pillow, but I felt like any chance of falling asleep was now lost for the night.

When a *ping, ping, ping* sounded against my windowpane thirty minutes later, I told myself it was either rain (in October? In Thurman Oaks?) or my imagination.

A thud that nearly shattered the glass, however, made my heart catapult to my throat. I threw back the covers and crept to the window. Pulling back the shade, I crouched down on one knee and cupped my hand to the glass.

Outside, moonlight shone down on a tall, dark figure a few feet from my window. Not a stranger or a potential strangler. But a guy offering a sweet smile.

Omigod, what was Jared doing here?

Shock tangled with some very mushy girl feelings that I'd deny to my last breath, and I flipped the lock and cranked the window ajar. "Jared?"

"I got your message," he called out softly. "Didn't want to wake your mom by calling."

"It wasn't important," I shout-whispered.

"Come outside."

I knew I should tell him—*Alison's brother*—to go home. That it was late. And my relationship with his sister was complicated enough. But since when did I let my good sense guide my actions?

"Be right there!"

Dressed in PJ pants and a tank top, I crept down the hallway, flipped on the porch light, and cruised out the front door. Goose bumps rose on my bare arms, and my feet did a squish-squash thing in the dewy grass. I couldn't remember feeling happier.

He stood on the lawn, moonlight dancing off his dark hair. Looking big and strong and impossibly handsome. I moved closer and closer until his voice jarred me from my steamroller advance.

"Hey," he said in a low murmur. "What's up?"

I paused, maybe a foot away, and tried to collect myself. After all, *I'd* called *him*.

"This sounds sort of dumb now, but I couldn't sleep and really just wanted a friend."

He just stood there, giving off this amazing mix of superhot masculinity and protective tenderness. I almost *wanted* to unload on him, just to have his dark eyes, his focus, all over me.

But the thing was, suddenly I didn't feel like talking. Like overanalyzing. Like being friends.

I knew what I wanted was . . . *this*. Jared and me, alone in the darkness. The only two people in the world. Making everything and everyone else go away . . .

I inched closer.

As if in answer to my prayers—or maybe because we really *were* in sync—his hands moved to my bare upper arms (*Oh god, kiss me! Kiss me!*), and his face angled toward mine.

My heart went into overdrive.

(Would he hear it?)

(Would he feel it?)

His mouth then covered mine.

Yes!

Soft lips, soft kiss.

I tippy-toed up closer to him, deepening the kiss, giving him my all. And taking from him his very best.

Then after a couple of minutes he broke the kiss, slung an arm across my shoulder, and led me toward his mom's SUV. Where he pressed his backside against his hood, and pulled me close.

Warmth spread through me. From the engine. From him.

"Holding you feels so good," he said, his voice rumbling through me.

Tucking my face into his neck, I made a *mmm* noise. Part agreement, part *yum!*

"You may be small, Nic, but every *inch* of you is sexy. I've been hung up on you as long as I can remember."

I pulled back to stare into his eyes. Dark, shimmery. "You're kidding."

"Hardly. But it wasn't until I saw you with that guy on the beach that I knew it. I've never been so jealous in my entire life. Made me realize why I'd been in such a bad mood all those hours I drove you around to buy a dress to wear with . . . *him*."

I laughed. I mean, it wasn't funny, but it made me so darned *happy* to hear this. "I'm sorry. Especially because I didn't know at the time you and Rascal hated each other."

"We hated each other all right. Because of you."

"Me?"

"Of course. I mean, his bragging always bugged me. But didn't make me insane until he started talking about you."

I studied the planes of his face in what little light emanated from the porch lamp. "So the threats? The punches? The broken windows?"

"You. You. You."

A smile spread across my face. I was the kind of girl that guys got all worked up over!

But my elation was short-lived when my ever-active mind took hold. Jared wasn't doing what Rascal had tried to do, was he? Win me as some sort of twisted grand prize?

I squinched my eyes. "I guess *this* makes you the official winner, huh?"

"That battle's already over," he said, and frowned. "It's just me chasing you now. And I'm more determined than ever. I want to go out with you, Nic, to be your boyfriend."

Be still, my heart!

After a breath and a hell-yeah smile on my part, his mouth found mine again.

And I wondered if love could be this simple. A series of perfect moments that go on and on . . .

"And I want you to go with me to the homecoming dance," he said when our faces pulled apart.

I pressed my palm against his and folded my fingers with his. I wanted that more than anything, too. But first, I had to be sure of something.

"Nothing to do with my dress, right? With feeling sorry for me because I haven't gotten to wear it? With feeling sorry for me, period?"

"Nothing. For all I care, you can wear the same bikini you're going to wash my car in."

I swatted him. "When are you going to forget about me washing your car?"

"Never."

He grinned, and I squeezed his hand.

"You know what, Jared McCreary? My dress and I would *love* to go to the homecoming dance with you."

My mom appeared in the doorway a few minutes later. "Nicolette?" she called in a harsh whisper. "What in the *world* are you doing out there?"

Still pressed against Jared, I kept my tone down, too. "Jared and I are just talking, Mom!"

"Can't you talk tomorrow? In the *daylight*?"

"Be right there!"

He released his hold on my waist and inched a respectable distance away. "Call me when you wake up."

My thoughts spun. In all the heady excitement, I'd completely and totally forgotten the Alison angle. It had to be handled delicately, not just a "So guess what? I'm with your brother now."

I frowned. "Um, maybe you better call me. When Alison's not around."

His lips pressed into a hard line. "Yeah, we'll work on that. I took care of Mitch and Harrison and those guys, didn't I?"

I nodded. I hadn't gotten a call or a long look from one of them in days.

"Okay," I answered. I guessed if I was going to trust the guy, now would be as good a time as any.

We shared quick good-nights, and I ran on tippy-toes across the wet grass, carrying enough feelings/thoughts/worries to rival my body weight. Still, when I met Mom in the doorway, I threw myself into her surprised arms.

"I'm going to the homecoming dance with Jared!"

She quietly closed the door. "That's wonderful, honey. But I didn't realize you even liked him."

Where had Mom been?

With no interest in attempting sleep, I plopped on the couch and spilled. I told her everything—about Jared, his windshield, Kylie, and my talk with Coach Luther.

"Nicolette, I never thought I'd say this, but you're getting more like your father every day."

I drew in a gasp. "Mom . . ."

"No, but in a good way. You both go headfirst into things, not always knowing what you're doing, but determined. And one way or another, you land on your feet. I could learn from the two of you."

"Mom," I said, getting off the couch. "Come on, you're perfect just the way you are."

She leaned over and kissed my forehead. "I'm a work-in-progress. But you? I wouldn't be surprised if you make all your dreams come true. When you set your mind to something, you make it happen." She tousled my hair. "In any case, it sounds like you've found the perfect use for your prom dress."

I let out a blissful sigh. "I have, haven't I?"

Top Ten Uses for an Unworn Prom Dress

#2

**Wear it to the homecoming dance,
with the RIGHT date—the guy you didn't
even realize you bought it for.**

Two things were abundantly clear to me the next morning:

(a) I was deliriously happy over Jared;

(b) I was seriously worried over Alison.

So, doing a one-eighty spin on what I'd told Jared, I picked up the phone and called the McCreary house.

He answered, and to my shock and relief, still sounded happy. After trading silly, gushy words that I would die before repeating, he told me Alison was in her room.

"Good. Tell her I'm coming over." I bit my lip. "No—don't. Just keep her there, okay?"

My mom drove me over, and suddenly there I was—pressing the intercom box at the end of the Mc-Crearys' gated drive. My knees practically knocking.

Alison answered.

"Hey," I managed, "it's Nic."

"Nic?" But she seemed more surprised than upset.

After an endless pause (longer than the run to the car in the pouring rain after you blow-dried your hair, but shorter than, say, making hot fudge on the stove), the buzzer blasted at me and the electronic gate rolled back.

She met me at the door. Wearing boxers, a T-shirt, and a half smile. "You okay?" Concern glowed in her eyes.

A good sign. Very good. If she'd wanted me to rot in hell, she wouldn't be standing here, looking all . . . well, concerned.

"Yeah. I—I just wanted to come by and see you."

We moved into their family room and plopped down on the couches running along one wall.

I started. "Some of the things we've been saying lately—and not saying—well, things have gotten too weird between us." I stopped and sort of held my breath, praying she'd agree, that she'd make this easy. Well, easier.

"Yeah," she said, to my profound relief. She

shrugged; then a smile touched her mouth. "I'm glad you're here. I don't want things to be weird, either."

She went on to tell me how she'd spent yesterday afternoon alone at the library. "Can you believe my English teacher demands actual *book references* on the term paper? Seriously!"

I laughed with her, probably too hard. I loved that she had been studying, that she hadn't been doing something fun without me.

"One good thing, though," she went on. "Chas Zachary was sitting at another cubicle. You know, that hottie from my English class? Well, I kept sneaking looks his way, and I *swear*, half the time he was looking back!"

We giggled and speculated about his interest. I couldn't help thinking how wonderful it would be for her (okay, and for me) if she hooked up with him. But I also knew that life wasn't always that simple.

"And you know," she said, "Chas is on the soccer team with Mitch. We could double-date. Don't suppose he ever called you?"

Mitch. Ugh. "Yeah, a couple times."

"And you didn't tell me?"

"Nothing much to say." I slipped my ring over my knuckle and back. "I'm sure you heard those friends with benefits rumors going around about Jared and me? Mitch was trying to cash in."

She frowned. "Okay, he's toast. Forget I brought him up." She pressed her lips together. "And speaking of forgetting, could you forget the hard time I've been giving you about Rascal lately? I know he's history, and I probably shouldn't have told you all that stuff. At least not the way I did. I'm sorry."

I could forgive her—because I was pretty sure her anger was fixated on Rascal so she didn't have to think about Jared and me. Which really had been happening. Whether or not I had wanted to admit it. So I managed a nod.

"Look," she said, and jumped up. "I need to take a shower. Come on back to my room and hang out. Then we'll go over to the mall, okay? My parents are out, but we'll get Jared to drive."

Jared. Oh, yeah. *Him.*

At the mention of her incredible brother, I bit down on my lip, then told her (somewhat vaguely) that there was some stuff we should probably talk about.

"Sure," she said, and veered into her room. "We have all day."

I hoped we did. After I dropped my bomb.

•

Soon I was cross-legged on her floor, flipping through a *Teen People* like I'd done a gazillion times before. Water thundered out of the shower pipes in Alison's private bath, making a whooshing sound that was almost soothing to the ear, but absolutely no help in readying me for the Talk.

I told myself that a selling point was that Jared

was a much better boyfriend for me than Rascal. I could just say: *See how much my taste has improved?* But I didn't really see that flying.

Suddenly, I felt a shift in the air. I glanced toward the door.

Slouched in the doorway, Jared was backlit by windowed sunshine. "Hey."

My heart went dancing. "Hey yourself."

Without even thinking, I jumped up. He met me a couple of steps in and lowered his head. But instead of kissing me, he grinned and pressed his nose against mine.

I smiled back, a twinge of pain the only reminder of my volleyball mishap. It became an unspoken contest. Whose smile was biggest. Silliest. Longest. Without laughing.

I tried concentrating on the sound of the falling water, on the beating of my own heart, on not cracking up. I would *win*.

Maybe if I reached out and tickled him. Maybe—

The bathroom door opened.

"Nic, did I leave my—"

Alison!

I jumped away from Jared like I'd been splattered with hot oil, and turned toward my best friend, my eyes shock-wide.

Dressed in a terry-cloth robe, her red hair still dry, Alison stared at us, her mouth curled cruelly. "Oh, isn't *this* just great? In my own *room*, no less! And yeah, Nic, *sure* you came to see me."

"I did!" I said, leaping toward her. "Jared and me . . . well, that happened last night. Today was totally about seeing you, telling you, making sure you were okay with us going out."

Her eyes narrowed. "Well, I'm *not* okay. I'm not. Uh-uh, this is just . . . too creepy."

Monkey in the Middle

"That's totally unfair," I said, so softly that I didn't even know if my words had hit the air.

"Alison," Jared said. "Come on . . . give us a break."

I shook my head to silence him. I was grateful that he'd tried to help. But this was between Alison and me.

He gave me a nod and disappeared.

"How do you think *I* feel?" she spat, yanking the belt on her terry-cloth robe so tight she looked like she was in pain. "You've been my friend since seventh grade. Every time you've called, come over, gone to the beach house with us—everything. It's been because you want to be with me.

"Now I don't know what to believe. Will you be coming by for me or for my brother? It's like I'm not good enough for you anymore or something."

"Nothing has to change between us," I said lamely.

"Oh, yeah? Well, you're sure as hell going to need another best friend if you want to gush about how cute he is. Or complain when he ignores you or forgets your birthday. Or God forbid, if you want to talk about your sex life!"

Got me there.

"And then what happens if you break up?" she went on. "And you hate his guts? So you don't come around here at all anymore? Suddenly I'm caught in the middle? Or do I get dumped, too?"

"No," I said, emotion welling in my throat. "No, Alison."

"Or one of you starts cheating or plotting a split? And I'm put in the position of keeping secrets?"

She had clearly put *waaay* more thought into this than I had. I'd just been bumbling along, letting my feelings guide me, trying to make heads or tails out of my life.

Which was where Jared had come in. Making me smile, knocking me back into the box when I got too crazy. Helping my life make sense.

Was that so bad? How often did you find someone who not only set your heart on fire, but did wonderful things with your head, too?

Her face was a thundercloud, emotions flashing like lightning. Anger, sadness, hope.

"You've made really good points," I admitted. "Things I haven't thought through. But it seems to me that we've been through harder things, and if we try real hard . . ."

Her expression went stiff. Unrelenting. Telling me I had to choose.

The thing was, there was no choice. Alison was a one-in-a-million friend. She'd stood by me through everything. The problems with my family, guys, Coach Luther. She'd believed in me. Even when I hadn't believed in myself. I couldn't turn my back on her.

Jared . . . would have to wait. Or understand. Or both.

As would The Dress . . . apparently destined to live for eternity in its bag behind my door.

"Okay," I said, and shrugged.

"Okay, what?"

"Okay." I swallowed hard. "I won't go out with Jared."

Her brow creased. "You won't?"

"No." I tried to come up with a smile but couldn't find one. I felt like I was falling into a dark, bottomless hole, spiraling further and further from the light. But Alison was falling right alongside me. Wasn't she?

"You were in my life first. You've been there when I've needed you. If it means that much to you, I won't be with him."

She studied my face, as if searching for the truth. "Yeah?"

"Yeah," I managed.

"Okay. Okay, good." She looked a little stunned, standing there for a minute or so like she didn't believe me, then mumbled, "Uh . . . I'm going to get in the shower. Then we'll go do something. Like we planned."

She closed the bathroom door behind her.

I wilted onto her bed. Wanting to cry. To scream. To hit something.

Wanting *my best friend*. So I could huff and sigh and roll my eyes and tell her all about this unfair and terrible predicament. And wait for her to tell me everything I wanted to hear, like how it was going to be all right.

But that *so* wasn't going to happen.

I'd have to pull myself back together all by myself. I couldn't rely on Alison. And I especially couldn't count on Jared. Not after I released this newest bomb.

Like a sleepwalker, I padded through the living room, kitchen, family room, and out to the attached garage. The garage door was up, and sunlight and a light breeze filtered in across the pavement. Guy-sized sneakers and blue jeans stuck out from under a Camaro. (With fully intact windows, I noticed.)

I waited, collecting my thoughts. And my nerve. Then, finally, "Jared."

His torso and head rolled into view. "Hey. You two work things out?"

"Everything's going to be fine," I spoke, monotone. "As long as I don't have anything to do with you."

"What? You didn't agree to that, did you?" He bolted up. "That's crap!"

I must have looked as distraught as I felt, because his face suddenly softened, and he moved toward me. I buried my head in his shoulder and for the second time in less than two weeks I spurted waterworks at him. Tears blinded my eyes and choked my throat.

His arms came around me. Strong, protective, caring. Feeling so good, I didn't even care how lame I seemed.

"Aw, come on, Nic. Don't give up."

Tears sliding down my cheeks, I let out a sob.

"Come on," Jared said, and stroked my hair. "It'll be okay."

I didn't deserve him. Here I was trying to throw him away, and he was "being there" for me. I buried my face in his chest.

Alison's voice suddenly cut through the haze that was my brain. I sniffed, wiped the tears from my eyes, dislodged myself from her brother's arms, and turned to her.

Robed, a towel twisted over her wet hair, she had

swollen eyes, too. Crazy as it seemed, I couldn't help thinking that was the fastest shower on record. There was no way she'd used conditioner.

"I'm the one," she choked out, looking at me.

I shook my head.

"You know, Kylie and the digital picture." She swallowed hard. "That day you went to your dad's. Kylie saw you leaving and came up to me. Wanting to know if you two were a couple, what the story was." Wincing, she continued. "I told her he was just taking you to your dad's, no big deal. She started saying all this stuff about how you'd been using me all these years to get close to my brother. How you don't care about girls' feelings, only guys', which is why you tried to steal her boyfriend."

"That's not true!" I wailed.

She nodded, her movement slow and strained. "I got mad. At her. At you, for putting me in that situation, and mad at myself for buying into it. Next thing I knew, I was telling her about the beer picture, and how I'd use it against you if I had to. Which was just stupid, just something to say. I mean, you and I know it was to keep you away from Rascal, not Jared, but she didn't, right? Anyway, I'd already deleted it. She never had a copy. The *nerve* to try to *blackmail* you."

I shifted my weight, swimming through a wave of thoughts and emotions. Alison had betrayed me. Sort of. I wanted to be mad. Ticked off. Irate.

Unfortunately, I wasn't always the Great Seer of

the Big Picture, either. I'd blurted out dumb things. Who was I to judge?

"I'm sorry," Alison said, and teared up herself. "I never thought I'd be the kind of friend who'd backstab."

"You didn't," I said gently, and smiled. "Not really. It just goes to show that neither one of us is perfect." I leaned in for a hug, and pulled back to see her trying to smile.

"Some friend I am, huh, Nic? I rat you out, then tell you to choose between Jared and me. I was so sure you'd choose him. So I could just be mad, and I wouldn't have to feel guilty anymore."

I took a moment to let her words register. "You don't have to feel guilty. I should have been more sensitive to what you were going through, too."

Her gaze swept from me to Jared and back again. "You guys are probably perfect for each other. But can you understand how this feels to me? It's like I'm losing my best friend."

I patted her arm. "Could you give this a try, Alison? I promise you I'll have time for a boyfriend *and* a best friend. And if I do something stupid," I said, and dropped my voice to a low whisper, as if Jared couldn't hear, "like start to tell you how great your brother is, you have my full permission to whack me upside the head."

She sniffed and smiled.

He smirked.

Relief did a volcano thing inside me. . . . I half

expected hot air and confetti to blow out the top of my head.

And can I tell you how much I wanted to put this whole thing behind us and just go to the mall?

•

Jared played chauffeur. But on the way home, he dropped Alison off first. She didn't seem to mind, just said she'd call me later. And I was glad for time alone with Jared.

The best thing about having a sucky life was how sweet it was when it suddenly improved.

I floated inside the house, intending to update my mom on the newest developments. But Mom wasn't alone. Dad was there. With Autumn. And some strange suitcases, clogging up the hallway.

Was I hallucinating—or did Mom have the bigger update?

"Your dad and Autumn are going to spend a couple of nights with us while looking for their own place near here."

Say what?

"I was offered a job in L.A.," Dad said from the couch. "Your mom's been nice enough to let me crash here," he added, and patted a seat cushion. "And we thought maybe you could make space for Autumn in your room?"

Thoughts clashed like cymbals in my head. "Yeah, I guess, but what about Caffeine? Uh, Cathleen?"

"We've separated," Dad said. He glanced toward his other daughter, who was happily shredding one of Mom's old *Martha Stewart Living* magazines. "Cathleen agreed it was best that Autumn go with me."

I stared at the black-haired toddler. The baby who'd been born to infuriate me. To replace me. If my dad was the best parent she had—well, she didn't have much, did she?

Poor thing.

My mom took a couple of steps closer. "Your dad and I worked out an arrangement. Until I'm reinstated at work, or decide what it is I'm going to do, I'm going to be Autumn's day-care provider. In turn, he'll cover our mortgage."

That was the goofiest thing I'd ever heard. Mom and Autumn?

My face must have given me away, because Mom excused the two of us and pulled me into the kitchen. "This is a financial arrangement, Nicolette. It allows me to stay home and reassess my career. I'm not looking at Autumn as my ex-husband's daughter, but as your half sister, who has had a tough break, and needs some help."

Her gaze sharpened. "But that's it, you understand? In a few days, they'll move out. She'll come and go here at the house. But your dad and I will never get back together."

I nodded. I'd let that dream go ages ago. I was just glad Mom was making strides toward putting her life back together.

Meanwhile, I supposed I could try to be nice.

"Come on, Autumn," I said, moving back into the living room and offering my hand. "I've got even better magazines to rip up in my room. Magazines full of cute guys."

To my surprise, she slipped her tiny hand inside mine and came with me. It was sort of sweet. Her footsteps barely made any noise as we padded down the hallway and into my room.

"What that?" she asked, turning and pointing at the garment bag on the back of my door.

Ha! She sure *was* my sister. She could feel the pull of The Dress even through the plastic.

"Only the most beautiful prom dress—uh, homecoming dress—in the entire world."

"I see! I see!"

I twisted my ring. She was one of the last people in the world I felt deserved that treat. But hey, things weren't always as they seemed. Mom and Dad were friends. Alison and I were best friends again. Jared and I were *more* than friends.

Guess there was room for an upgrade in my sister relationship, too.

I got down on one knee. "Okay, kiddo, but first we wash your hands." A closer look showed a peanut butter—colored smear on her shirt, and what looked like blue marker on her arm. "Better make it a full bath."

"I wear it!"

"It's a gazillion sizes too big for you, Autumn."

But it's just right for me, I thought, steering her toward the bathroom. I knew that for a fact—I'd tried it on enough. I'd danced in it, sung ballads in it, cried in it. The Dress molded to my body like a second skin, like someone had made it exclusively for me.

And for a dance that I hoped wasn't just about homecoming, but about new beginnings, too.

Dressed for Success

THREE WEEKS LATER

Some people were disappointed that the homecoming dance didn't have a live band or a cutting-edge light system.

Not me.

Nothing could spoil my perfect evening. Not the canned music, not the crappy food, not the high-level security of teachers and parents making sure no couples got close on the dance floor, let alone got jiggy. But I was too busy shaking my dress and my stuff. In the small space between Jared's tuxedoed body and heaven.

It didn't get any better than this—or so I thought.

The DJ's voice cut through the speakers. "We have a request for an oldie," he said, and the overhead lights flickered a couple of times. "From one best friend to another." Without a musical intro came the oh-so-familiar voice of Paul McCartney.

A laugh snaked its way up my throat, and I scanned the sea of faces for a particularly familiar one, undoubtedly smiling under her beauty-parlor halo of red curls.

Jared pulled me and my scrumptious layers of crinoline to his chest. One hundred percent oblivious to the song's pity party significance to me. And driving home the fact that even though Jared and I had been A Recognized Couple for almost a month, Alison and I still had our best-friend secrets.

His body moved in rhythm with the music, with me, with my heart. Snuffing out the painful memories by making new ones.

I closed my eyes. No more thinking.

When the song ended, I opened them to see Alison smirking at me. "I thought you'd like that," she said, and grabbed my arm, laughing. "Come on, let's go to the girls' room."

A doubtful frown creased Jared's brow, and he looked at Alison's date, Chas Zachary. (After making next to no official progress with Chas, Alison had finally asked *him* to the homecoming dance. And he'd been hanging on her like a lovesick puppy ever since. Which goes to show that sometimes crushes are made, not born.)

"Why do I feel like I'm missing something?" Jared asked Chas.

Chas shrugged.

Alison's smile widened. "Girl stuff."

I gave Jared's arm a be-right-back squeeze and followed her through the gyrating bodies.

The cool hallway air was a welcome relief on my skin, but the bathroom was packed, with some girls primping in front of sinks and mirrors, others in a wiggling line for the stalls. Still, it was fun to see everyone so decked out, to examine one another's dresses in full light.

While we waited, Alison told me that Harrison had gotten his butt thrown out for being drunk. I hadn't seen it but didn't doubt it, either. I'd smelled alcohol on a bunch of people tonight.

Which was plain stupid to me. Was it really worth the risk of being thrown out?

A stall opened. A vision in fluffy lavender emerged—in a dress so captivating that it took me several seconds to glance at the face attached to it. To recognize Zoe.

"Omigod, Zoe, you look so beautiful!" I gushed, and gave her a quick hug.

She beamed. "So do you!"

I leaned in, lowering my voice to confidentially low. "I'm so glad the dance worked out for you."

She smiled. "Almost didn't. The dress, I mean." She leaned in closer. "I got lucky—"

A retch and spew from inside one of the stalls stopped our conversation—and all noise. Gazes raced around the bathroom. Arched brows. Smiles. And then names being silently mouthed.

I nudged Alison. She shrugged.

Then a voice, high and loud. "My dress! Oh God, my dress!" The stall door cracked open.

Heath Ledger himself couldn't have pulled me from my front-row seat. I was pretty sure I recognized that voice. . . .

Kylie staggered out, wiping her mouth with the back of her hand. Littered over a beaded top and flowing chiffon were brown stains and . . . chunks. "This is a disaster, a frigging disaster!" she slurred. "What if I'm homecoming queen?"

I laughed. Out loud. Then covered my mouth. Real quick. And then I turned to Alison. "Where's your camera phone *now*?"

Alison giggled.

Kylie shot us both a look, then swayed toward the mirror. "Rascal and I *will* win, you know."

"Oh," Alison said, holding back another laugh. "I don't doubt that. Chunky."

We laughed again. We couldn't help it.

Kylie fixed us with her best squint. But with her

makeup all smeared into raccoon eyes, she looked more pathetic than mean.

Alison moved into the empty stall. I followed Zoe out into the hallway.

"You were saying," I said. "About your dress?"

"Oh, I found a foundation that collects and recycles them. My mom and I went to their shop and I tried on a whole bunch. Of course, when I found this, I knew it was *it*."

She smiled, and I did, too.

"Anyway, it was totally free. I can keep it if I want, or return it. Isn't that incredible?"

"Incredible," I agreed.

"I'm going to take it back. I know it sounds crazy, but knowing I'm part of something bigger—sharing it with other girls who are going through hard times—actually makes me like the dress even more."

Crazy? Crazy wonderful.

These past months had been among the hardest I'd known. How could I have gotten through some of those moments without The Dress? To the naked eye, it was just material and thread. But to me, it had become a coping mechanism—even a friend.

Tonight was my dream come true—but I hadn't thought about what I'd do with my pink dream tomorrow. I just knew the bag was coming off the back of my door. That it was time to move on.

"Call me before you go," I said impulsively.

"Why? You want to come?"

"Yeah. I think I do. Me and my dress."

Because suddenly, there was *no doubt* that I'd found the final and totally right use for my dress.

Top Ten Uses for ~~an~~ a ~~Unworn~~ worn Prom Dress

#1

Donate it to a dress recycling charity so your dress can make some other girl as deliriously happy as it has made you.

Which, you know? Would be perfect. Just perfect.

AUTHOR'S NOTE

Do you have a "kindly worn" prom dress in *your* room?

Why not do as Nicolette and countless other girls have done and pass it on to a charitable dress recycling program?

Open up your heart and donate the dress that stole yours. Help another girl who might otherwise have to miss her homecoming, Spring Fling, or prom look and feel like a million dollars, too.

Come on . . . you can do it!

Call local used-clothing stores and ask about nearby prom dress recycling programs. Or type the words "prom dress" + "recycle" + the name of your closest city into an Internet search engine.

Or better yet, do as some heroic teens have done in their communities and start your own prom dress charity! Be a leader. Keep the good times going, starting with your prom dress.

Tina Ferraro spent much of her high school days people-watching, which didn't do much for her grades but later proved one of her better mistakes. A longtime resident of Southern California, she lives with her husband and their three kids. She loves to travel and can ask where the bathroom is in many languages. This is Tina's first novel for young readers. Visit her at www.tinaferraro.com.